THE FIESTA MURDERS

David E Burke

Also by the Author

Blue Murder
Book one in the Menorca Detective Series

This is a work of fiction. Names, characters, businesses, places, events, locales, and incidents are either the products of the author's imagination or used in a fictitious manner. Any resemblance to actual persons, living or dead, or actual events is purely coincidental.

For LEO.

You are forever in our hearts.

Author's note:

Every year, throughout the summer months, Menorca hosts a series of traditional Fiestas. These take place at different locations around the island, and are lively affairs filled with music, dance, and celebration.

The Fiestas feature performances in superior horsemanship from the Caixers and their magnificent Menorcan steeds. It is a unique island tradition that goes back a long way.

Menorca is unique in its cultural history - from the ancient days of the Moors whose architectural influence can be seen in the beautiful buildings at Ciutadella - to the British who occupied the place several times and left behind Gin, Bay windows, and some iffy Tricorn hats. Oh, and the French who tried to own it. And the Spanish who still do.

They are a very welcoming people and happy for visitors to share in their celebrations.

But even though it is a Balearic island, Español is not necessarily their first language.

Menorcans are proud of their Catalan heritage and identity and you will often see Catalan words on road signs, shops and other buildings, and hear conversations in a variety of tongues.

As such, I have used both Spanish and Catalan, and Menorcan idioms in this book. Simply to reflect the true nature of the Menorcan culture and spoken word.

CONTENTS

With thanks to my wife for her excellent feedback and considerable editing skills. Without which this book would not be as good as it should be.

SLAUGHTER OF THE RAG DOLLS

Every Easter Sunday in a sports field near the edge of a
Menorcan town, you will find full-sized and crudely made
effigies of local public figures. They are created especially
for an event known as *Matances de Bujots* or *Slaughter of
the Rag Dolls*. It's also known colloquially as *Shoot the
Guy*.

These *Rag Dolls* are made from old clothes stuffed with
straw, and they are usually meant to represent a local
dignitary or someone of standing in the community who has
been caught in a scandal of some sort. Or is just plain
unpopular.

These crude caricatures are replete with 'faces' - paper
masks with exaggerated features of the chosen victims
drawn on them.

Sometimes it is a prominent policeman, or a local
councillor. Usually because they are not very popular in the
community. Often, it is the Mayor, for no other reason than

the usual gripes concerning the local council's inept handling of everything from road repairs to tax hikes.

Typically, the event goes like this: each Easter Sunday, everyone who wishes to take part in this peculiar activity gathers in a field at the edge of town, armed with pistols and rifles loaded with blanks - to avoid any accidents. They form a rough semi-circle at suitable distance from their targets which are tied onto wooden posts. Then, at the stroke of 12 noon, they begin to 'shoot' en-masse at the half dozen or so effigies.

They walk slowly in unison towards the hapless figures, firing their weapons until they are at point-blank range. The idea being that, when they are very close, the sparks from the guns discharge will set the straw of the 'Rag Dolls' on fire. When this happens, they all stand back and watch them burn. Dancing, singing, drinking and clapping.

This year, there was a very round and well-stuffed 'Guy' dangling from the ropes that tied it to the wooden 'T' frame. Some said it was a very realistic representation of Mayor Alfonso. Others said it wasn't nearly fat enough.

With its masked sackcloth head, wearing the crudely drawn mayor's face complete with moustache and glasses, it looked very comical. Many joked that despite its grotesque appearance, it was actually better looking than the Mayor himself!

Miguel Aguilar had an axe to grind. His property tax was going to be increased again. It was already crippling him financially. So much so that his small butcher's shop business was on its last legs.

Not that his business was doing badly per-se, despite the new Supermercado having a well-stocked and competitively priced meat counter. No, many local people preferred to patronise his shop and buy their weekly pork, lamb and chickens from him as it was all fresh island produce and not imported like the big store.

The problem was those greedy bastards in the council had bumped up commercial premises rents another 7% this year, on top of rises in the four subsequent years, making it even more difficult to keep small businesses like his going. Despite his many letters to the Alcalde's Office and protestations at public meetings, his pleas for clemency by way of a tax reduction or rates freeze had fallen on deaf ears. And the Mayor was the worst of the lot.

He raised his shotgun and took aim at the pink heart drawn on the 'Mayor's' chest.

He wasn't on his own.

Xavier Mendes took careful aim with his pistol. He'd had plenty of practice this year shooting rats in his feed store. True, he could have laid down poison. Rats will eat anything. But he decided a quick and merciful end was far better for the pests than a slow painful death. And anyway, shooting them was much more satisfying. Especially if he imagined that the rats were the local town councillors. So, it was easy now to imagine that the Mayor was the biggest rat of them all. His gun may be firing blanks, but he felt it would be some kind of payback.

At the stroke of 12 noon, a shout went up and all hell broke loose. Round after deafening round was fired.

Slowly, the group of shooters walked forward in a closing circle towards the dummies, firing, reloading and firing again. The stifling smell of cordite filling the air.

The shooting stopped suddenly, as did the crowd when they drew near and the smoke began to clear. Silence fell as two things became evident: One: There was blood oozing from the bullet holes in the Mayor's portly puppet. And Two: Not everyone had been firing blanks.

The silence was shattered by shouts and screams.

Someone ran forward and pulled the blood-soaked mask from the effigy's head.

More screams rend the air as a real human face was revealed, the head lolling lifelessly, dead eyes staring in terror, mouth gagged with gaffer tape beneath a bloodied moustache.

Someone yelled for a doctor, but it was obvious to all that none could have survived the ferocious firing squad.

Not even the Mayor himself.

'ANOTHER DAY IN PARADISE?'

Frank Harmer stared glumly through the rain streaked patio doors and watched the wind tugging peevishly at the shrubs and small fruit trees that lined the walls of his garden. The weather had been like this for the best part of three weeks. Three long miserable and cold weeks. Unusual for late Spring in Menorca, but not unprecedented. Not in an El Niño year like this one.

He sighed heavily, stood up and began to stretch. A sharp pain lanced through the top half of his right leg. He swore and then sighed again as it subsided. That old bullet wound – a souvenir from his time on the force – was from an incident that had earned him a commendation for bravery and left him with a shattered knee that took years to mend. It often plagued him when the weather turned cold and damp. He laughed at the irony of it. He had moved out here to Menorca for its drier and warmer climate.

Of course, Paradise is often an illusion; there is always a downside, a snake in the grass.

The hard truth is that Menorca, despite it being a sunshine holiday destination, can in winter sometimes be wet, cold and very damp indeed.

The island is prone to high humidity. It's not a problem in the summer. That just makes sleeping a little uncomfortable on the warmest nights. But in winter it can mean extreme damp inside buildings. And most Menorcan buildings, particularly villas, are not really built for such conditions. They are fine in the sunny summer days when you can just throw open all the doors and windows and let the warm summer breezes sort it all out. But in the winter, when you tend to keep your doors and windows shut, the moisture can build up inside to very high levels.

Menorca holiday villa owners are used to this. They prepare their properties by wrapping their summer clothing and bedding in plastic bags for winter storage, and by leaving the windows open and shutters locked - especially if they intend to leave their houses empty for any length of time.

But it's not really an option if you are staying in your villa for the winter. If you are going to do so, it's a good idea to place dehumidifiers in the rooms that you are generally not using.

Frank was advised to do this by his neighbour and good friend Marisol. He was amazed to find that the dehumidifier's collectors were full of water and needed emptying every day, sometimes more than once.

The other thing about the colder winter months are the fuel bills. They can be astronomical for larger villas.

The trouble is that most of the older villas are poorly insulated and constructed of just a single skin of bricks and mortar. Neither do they have loft insulation as they don't have any lofts. You may have noticed on a Menorcan holiday that the ceiling is usually the underside of the roof.

As a result, Menorcan villas do not keep the heat in very well and, even on a winter's day with the temperature only just dropping into single figures, you will need to keep the heating on full blast. And that can cost a pretty packet in fuel bills. Even if it's supplemented by a traditional log-burning stove, as many Menorcan villa and country homes are, it doesn't save you much as the wood can be expensive to buy.

The trick, Frank learned, also from Marisol, was to seal off parts of the house and shut the heating off to those areas that aren't used so much for the duration of the winter. Just restrict yourself to living in and heating the main rooms that you use – i.e. the Kitchen, Lounge and master Bedroom.

He did try using the log burner. He had a ton of dried Olive Wood logs delivered - the kind favoured by Menorcans for their long slow burning qualities. However, an encounter with a large black Scorpion that was nesting in the woodpile put him off any repeat orders.

Frank winced at the memory and felt a shiver run down his spine. It had happened during a particularly cold spell and Frank had been waiting almost two weeks for his logs to be delivered. He had phoned the company several times to complain and each time was promised a delivery would be made 'mañana' - the *next day*.

It kept not happening. And, just when he had given up hope, while he was out shopping, the truck from the log company turned up unannounced and just dumped them on his drive.

When he returned, Frank was unable to get his car in and was faced with having to shift the entire load by hand to the store at the rear of his house.

He was sure the driver would be long gone, but looking around he saw the man and his truck were still there, waiting just down the road.

Evidently, he wasn't going anywhere until he got paid - in cash. Many small firms in Menorca like to be paid in cash.

The old guy was sat in his cab smoking and listening to the radio. He jumped and then grinned a stained gap-toothed smile when Frank wrapped angrily at the window. The driver got out and climbed down, still grinning as if he hadn't noticed the stormy look on Frank's face.

'Habla Inglés?' Frank enquired. He had learned the hard way not to assume everyone did in Menorca. In fact, outside the tourism industry, many people working in small shops and businesses on the island spoke very little or no English at all.

The Man shrugged. 'No señor. No Inglés.' He reached into his breast pocket and pulled out a grubby looking piece of paper and offered it to Frank 'You pay La Cuenta, sí?'

Frank stared stonily at it and then spoke. 'I've a bloody good mind not to pay you at all! I've been waiting for weeks and, I mean, look where you dumped the sodding things.' He turned and stabbed a finger at the huge pile of logs, taller than himself and spread across the entrance to his driveway. 'I mean, what is the point of dumping it all there? Eh?'

The man nodded and grinned happily as if he had just been complimented and said. 'Sí, es bueno. 350 euros.' He held out the receipt again and Frank snatched it from him.

He stared at it trying to think how to pay. He didn't have that much in cash on him or in the house. He had got it ready ages ago but had spent it bit by bit. He reached for his wallet and took out a credit card.

The man suddenly lost his smile. He ignored the proffered credit card, shook his head and said in very clear English. 'Cash only.'

From that point the transaction began to get heated. The man threatening to take back all his logs. Frank threatening to insert them in a place the man might find most disagreeable. It was on the point of really getting out of hand when a familiar voice broke the tension.

'Hay algún problema?'

They both turned and saw that it was Marisol.

The deliveryman gave her a smile and said. 'No pasa nada Señora. Este imbécil no tiene pasta.'

'Cuánto es?' Marisol enquired.

'350 Euros.'

Frank got the gist of this exchange and told her. 'Look, this idiot turns up 2 weeks late, dumps everything blocking my drive, and expects me to have 350 in cash. Moron!'

Although the man appeared not to understand all that Frank said, he clearly knew when someone was taking his name in vain. He gave Frank an angry look and took a step toward him, raising his small 5ft 5ins frame upward at the 6ft Brit and thrusting his chin forward.

Frank was half tempted to connect his fist with it.

Marisol, ever Frank's girl Friday, poured calm on the troubled waters and said in Spanish 'No problem. I have the money in cash, and I will go get it and pay you.'

The deliveryman looked delighted. She went into her house and quickly returned holding a wad of notes.

Frank had a face like thunder. 'What are you doing? I can't let you pay this twit for me.'

The man had a different view on things and held out his hand eagerly.

Marisol smiled a smile so sunny that the winter gloom seemed to disappear. She touched Frank's hand and said. 'No problema. What are friends for? I will pay this for you now.'

'But…but…'

'No arguments Señor Frank. You can give it to me later.'

Frank wondered if she really meant it to come out like that. But he couldn't say no to this lovely woman. A woman he had shared danger and adventure with and had come to regard as a very close and dear friend. A woman he had come to have feelings for.

Reluctantly, he acquiesced, and the transaction went ahead.

By now the driver was eager to get on his way and pick up another delivery. He hoped this time it would not be for another crazy and clearly cash-strapped Brit.

A SCORPION'S TALE

It was early evening by the time Frank got the last load into the wheelbarrow. It was backbreaking work transferring the huge pile of olive logs to the stack at the rear of his house. Marisol had offered to help but he wouldn't hear of it, saying it would be no trouble.

It was. It took the whole afternoon. He had just a small mound left as the evening sun began to set. It was then, just as he was placing them wearily into the wheelbarrow, that he noticed something small moving near his right foot. Something black and shiny. He couldn't quite make it out in the fading light and stooped to get a closer look.

He froze and felt a shiver of revulsion and fear run down his spine.

A Scorpion! A bloody buggering Scorpion! He had heard that they could be found out in the Menorcan countryside but were rarely seen in urban areas. Certainly, he had never seen one before outside of a zoo. This one must have been living happily out there in some woodland when some hairy-arsed bloke with a chainsaw came and chopped down his olive tree home and took it away to the lumber yard with him still in it.

Frank remained frozen in fear and disbelief. Surely, they treat this stuff for pests before delivery to their customers?

With a supreme effort of willpower, he moved his foot a little. The Scorpion turned to face him and raised its venomous tail over its shiny black body as if confronted by a foe. The creature was no bigger than a few inches in length, but it looked huge to Frank's terror filled eyes.

What should he do? Back away slowly? Jump away quickly? How fast could this thing move?

Perhaps if he just waited, not moving, the thing might decide he was no threat and just saunter off in search of another home. But that might take ages and it was getting darker and colder.

Now that the Scorpion had taken up a defensive posture, it seemed in no hurry to back down or move elsewhere. Worse, Frank's bad leg was beginning to cramp in the cold evening air. He knew he would have to move soon. He had visions of himself writhing in pain and dying alone in the dark from multiple Scorpion stings. Panic began to set in.

Just then he saw Theo, his neighbour's large tabby cat approaching.

He often popped over the wall to have a crafty crap in Frank's garden at this time of day. Curious, it saw the pile of logs and sauntered over. It had no fear of Frank, who often made a fuss of Theo and gave him tasty treats.

As Theo drew near, he caught sight of the Scorpion and

suddenly dropped into a crouch mode. Before the hapless insect could turn and prepare to defend against this new threat, the Cat had pounced, landing with his two front paws on its body. He gripped it firmly in his claws, and in a flash, with its sting flailing and pincers twitching, had the wriggling thing in his mouth. There was a sickly crunching sound and the deadly Arachnid stopped moving.

The cat shook it from side to side several times, let it fall triumphantly to the ground at his feet, in order to examine his kill.

Before it could do so, realising the thing might just be playing doggo and that Theo might be in danger, Frank picked up a handy looking log and finished it off with several sharp blows.

Theo was shocked by this and, deciding the Scorpion was no longer any sport, ran off to find fresh but less exotic game.

Frank breathed a huge sigh of relief and made a mental note to buy him some extra treats.

That was the last time he bought olive logs. Now he just kept the radiators on and decided to worry about the bills later. Occasionally, when he could be bothered to light the stove, he used the ready-made burning blocks that you could buy at the Trebaluger store. Okay, they were more expensive in the long run, but they came without any nasty surprises.

He winced once more at the memory, and then chuckled as he saw the funny side of it. Pouring himself a fresh cup of coffee he settled down to read the morning paper.

He always bought the Mallorca Daily Bulletin on his stroll to the store. It wasn't a Menorcan newspaper, but it did carry a good Menorca section. It was also in English.

He sipped his coffee, settled back and unfolded it. On the cover the headline screamed *'Local Mayor Killed in Tragic Easter Accident'.*

He read the feature with interest.

It was a terrible tragedy sure enough, but there was something that didn't quite add up. His copper's nose told him as much.

An *accident*?

Frank wasn't so sure. Too many coincidences. Too many people with motives. After all, the Mayor was unpopular according to Marisol.

Marisol! He wondered how she was doing in Madrid. She'd had to rush over there to deal with a family matter. She didn't go into detail, but seemed quite upset about it, so he didn't ask.

That had been two weeks ago, and he was missing her. More than he thought he should be. He missed her friendly smiling face, her musical laughter, and the smell of her perfume. Yes, they had the occasional nightly Skype call, but it wasn't quite the same.

He'd thought he had just been missing her companionship, but now...

He sat back, sighed wistfully and stared unseeing through the raindrops running down the pane, through the reflection of the thin, greying 60 year-old man with the sad face, and knew it might be more than that.

He wished something would happen to distract him. Some event to jolt him out of this melancholy mood. This damn weather didn't help.

Perhaps the phone would ring and it would be his friend Detective Inspector Juan, requesting his involvement to help solve another baffling crime.

He shook his head and dismissed the desire. That was wrong. He thought about the close brush with death that he and Marisol had the last time.

No. He had learned the hard way, you had to be careful what you wished for.

He made himself a fresh coffee and went back to reading the paper. Outside the rain began to ease.

A NEW BROOM

Juan Diego Rodriguez, Inspector Jefe of the Mahon Police department was not having a good day. In fact, he was not having a good week. Or month.

Not since the new boss was put in charge of his department. His old boss had taken 'early retirement' after that well-publicised case of smuggling and the murdered banker. Juan had cracked that case himself (with a little help from his good friend Frank Harmer) and had received a commendation for it. The framed certificate hung proudly on the wall behind his desk.

He recalled how that whole investigation had been suddenly brought to a halt half-way through on orders from his old boss. Of course, thanks to Frank Harmer's detective work, the case had a successful conclusion despite this. However, his old boss had come in for a lot of criticism of his handling of the case.

In the end, the top brass had decided that it was in

everyone's best interest to draw a line under the whole affair. Yes, just let the old man sail off into retirement. Sleeping dogs and all that.

In fact, he was sorry to see him go. He liked his boss's old-school no-nonsense approach to policing;'*Listen to your gut, don't jump to conclusions, break a few rules if you have to. Above all, trust your nose. If it smells rotten, then it is probably is.*'

Of course, he could be a little prickly at times. He didn't suffer fools and tended to speak his mind. He could be blunt, even cutting when dressing down an officer. But he was a fair man and always gave everyone a second chance, sometimes saying things like *'making cock-ups is how we learn'* and *'pain is our best teacher'*.

He commanded respect from the entire force. The junior officers lived in fear of him and nicknamed him 'The Dark Lord' and joked that wherever you were he had his 'evil eye' on you. But he kept everyone in line and the whole place running like clockwork.

However, he was a pussycat compared to this new Chief. One Magda Helena Volterra. She was a nightmare in comparison. Juan found her difficult to get on with from day one.

When he first heard the news of her arrival, he was quite pleased. Like him, she was coming from a large mainland city police force. So maybe she could help to stir things up and introduce some fresh ideas and methodologies. Goodness knows this place could do with a bit of a shake-up. Could benefit from joining the 21st Century.

Now he was regretting that wish. She was shaking things up

a bit too much.

On her first day she had assembled everyone in the main briefing room at 8am for the usual formal meet and greet.

It was a fine and sunny Spring morning. Everyone seemed in good humour. Chatting away about what they had done on the weekend, what their kids did, shopping trips etc… Then all went quiet as this diminutive figure entered the room attired in full dress uniform complete with pips, bravery medals and peaked hat adorned with the scrambled egg of senior rank.

Despite her lack of height and petite figure she still managed to project an aura of unquestionable authority. Especially when she spoke.

After a sweet toothy smile that lasted all of two seconds, she laid down the law. The commandments according Jefe Superior (Chief Inspector) Magda Helena Volterra.

She made it clear in no uncertain terms that there were going to be big changes around here. Root and branch. Top to bottom. Everyone in the Mahon Police Department was going to have to shape up and 'get a grip on things' hmmm?

She'd actually used that term. She had said it in a cold staccato manner, raising herself up to full 5-foot 3inches in height and, panning slowly around the room, staring into each of their faces, like a prison yard searchlight.

Her expression and tone declared that she was not someone to be messed with. Not a person whose wrath you would want to incur.

Despite this, Juan couldn't help laughing. Yes, she was

clearly capable and formidable in spite of her small stature. She could never have climbed so rapidly up the ranks if she hadn't been a force to be reckoned with.

No, it was the fact that she bore an uncanny resemblance to his old school form teacher Señora Fuentes. A lady of similar stature of whom he had very fond memories. She also had a formidable presence, much larger than her physical presence, but with a wicked sense of humour.

She often started out with a stern message when her class was getting disruptive, but soon made them laugh like drains with a brilliant joke before the end of the lesson.

Juan failed to hide his amusement. That was a mistake. One he would never make again. She mistook his innocent mirth for comment on her lack of height and fixed a laser-like stare on him. Everyone in the room felt uneasy.

'Something funny inspector...?' Here she leant forward and looked at his name tag... 'Rodriguez?'

Hoping to placate her, he held up his hands and smiling said. 'No Chief. Not at all. Please continue.'

She clearly took his smile to mean that he was still amused by her and gave him a withering look that said *'You will pay for that'.*

And he did. From that day on she made his life a living hell. She gave him the worst duties – putting him on night shifts and ordering him to search through and collate the mountain of ancient paper case files that lurked in the bowels of the basement file room.

It was a mess down there. It was also cold, dimly lit and damp. Worse, these files hadn't been properly ordered or even updated for decades. Most were badly typed and hand-written paper reports in cardboard folders and boxes.

Almost all were of minor misdemeanours and domestic feuds and petty crimes - someone had stolen another man's goat or pig. Builders were working on a Sunday. Neighbours disputing a *right of way*. There was even a recent report of a UFO seen over Mahon harbour!

So now he was working the *X Files*!

He would have laughed if he wasn't so fed up and frustrated. It was a Herculean labour to sort out all these files and then get them transferred into an electronic database. And guess who had to do all the data entry typing? Something he was not great at and used just two fingers. It would take an eternity.

After two weeks, it seemed that way.

So, he was delighted and surprised to be given a new case to investigate. One that would take him out of the 'dungeon' for a few days. Perhaps longer. Hopefully, for good. So, he was surprised and delighted when he was summoned for a briefing to the new Chief's office.

He gently tapped on her half open office door and stood waiting in the doorway. She had her head down and seemed engrossed in paperwork.

Without looking up she enquired 'Are you working on anything really important inspector?' She waived him in and pointed vaguely at the empty chair on the other side of her desk. He sat down and shook his head 'No ma'am. Not really.' and added with a sarcastic tone 'Just a little paperwork.'

She looked up, smiled flatly and slid a file across the desk. 'Good. I'd like you to investigate this. The press are calling it an unfortunate *accident*.' Here she made air quotes. 'I am sure that is the case, but we have to be seen to be carrying out a proper investigation.'

He opened the file. It was that tragic shooting business of the Mayor. Everyone had heard about it. There was a picture of the man standing proudly in his chains of office at some formal function, and two of his bloodstained and bullet-ridden corpse, one at the crime scene and one at the path lab.

He read the notes quickly and saw that though the prime cause of death was gunshot, the report was inconclusive as to how and why it happened. No-one had confessed to organising a 'prank gone wrong' as the newspaper speculated. And nobody had admitted using live ammunition.

Officially, foul play was not suspected.

It looked straight forward to Juan. It probably *was* an accident or a 'prank gone wrong'.

In which case he wondered why they were sending him, one of their most senior detectives and not a more junior officer to investigate? He looked up from the notes and enquired 'Am I missing something Chief? I mean, this does look like a case of death by misadventure. I am sure the guilty party will come forward and confirm that eventually.'

A thin smile played on her lips. She nodded at the file lying open on the desk. 'Take a look in the back pocket.'

He picked it up and looked in the cardboard pocket on the

inside back cover where extra notes were sometimes kept. He found a small clear plastic zip-lock envelope with a slip of paper inside.

He held the packet up in front of him to examine it more closely and saw that the small rectangular piece of paper had brown stains on it and a crudely drawn symbol. He turned it around through 360 degrees slowly and thought he recognised the shape. He looked quizzically at his new boss.

She shrugged. 'It was found on the victim. Any idea what it might mean?'

'Looks like a Mobius.'

She looked at him blankly.

'A mathematical symbol that represents infinity.'

There was contempt to her voice as she snapped 'And there was me thinking it was a number 8.'

He ignored her and looked at the brown stained piece of paper with the drawing on it once more. 'Okay. It's a number 8. Doesn't necessarily mean anything sinister. Could be a date or time or the number of a racehorse in the 3.30 at La Mancha. Just an odd bit of paper in the man's pocket, that's all.'

She seemed to take a delight in telling him the next bit. 'Oh, it wasn't found in his pocket. It had been placed in a body cavity!'

He let the evidence drop to the desktop.

She laughed out loud seeing his shock and discomfort.

Then she made a joke that Juan thought was in poor taste. 'So, if there is a crime here Inspector, I expect you to get to the *bottom* of it.'

He gave her a sickly smile and stood up, holding his sullied right hand out in front of him but making sure that his middle finger was pointing upright and in her direction. 'I'll get right on it.'

He hurried to the restroom and washed his hands repeatedly with the antibacterial soap. What a bitch!

Even so, he had to admit it was very strange. What did it mean? Who had put it there? The victim himself? No. Too absurd.

A 'message in a bottom?'

No. No more tasteless jokes. A poor unfortunate man had lost his life here.

He looked up as he dried his hands in a paper towel and caught his serious looking reflection in the mirror. It was a handsome face. Sure, there were a few lines around the eyes and on the forehead now, and the nut-brown hair had flecks of grey, as did his close-cropped beard.

But it was a friendly face that people found most agreeable, and he began to laugh despite his dislike of the new boss and his sullied hand.

So, she did have a sense of humour after all! Goodness knows you needed one in this job.

And a trip out to that town to investigate this case would at least get him out of the basement for a while. Or forever if, unlikely though it was, this turned out to be a murder case! That would change things around here. Especially if he found out who the perpetrator was and brought them to justice.

After all, there were some very strange aspects to consider. Why was the Mayor bound and gagged? Why did he not struggle to attract help? And if the idea was to get him killed, how could the kidnapper be sure someone would be using live rounds?

Unless they did the deed and shot him themselves.

Thinking about it, none of that made sense really. It was too elaborate. Would it not have been simpler just to shoot the Mayor in the first place? Why go to so much trouble?

And what about that piece of paper the pathologist had found in the man's rectum?

He decided a bit of feedback would help him sort things out. Yes, he would give his good friend Frank Harmer a call. See if he could make any sense of it.

Maybe. In a day or two. After he had spent some time in the town investigating… interview some of the witnesses… enjoy a few nice meals… take some beach walks to think things through. No point in rushing these things.

He was waiting for the lift to take him down to the car park when he heard a familiar voice call from behind.

'Oh officer Rodriguez?'

He turned and saw Jefe Superior Volterra standing there holding up the plastic bag with the stained paper message inside. Behind her he could see that everyone in the staff squad room appeared to be watching. He thought he heard laughter. Some looked like they were smiling!

She was trying not to laugh herself and failed as she said loudly. 'Don't forget this piece of evidence that was removed from the victim's… mouth!'

The entire squad room erupted in raucous laughter.

The lift arrived with a loud ping. He got in and pressed the basement button. The laughter receded as the doors closed and the lift descended.

Then he started laughing loudly too.

He shook his head. She'd got him good.

'A VIEW TO DIE FOR'

About a square kilometre in size, the ancient stone military Fortress of La Mola sits atop a grassy hill on a peninsula of rugged land at the mouth of Mahon Harbour.

This imposing edifice was built in 1875 at the order of Queen Elizabeth II of Spain – the Spanish then being in control after taking Menorca back from the British.

It was strategically sited there to afford a clear 360 degree view out to sea. Its prime purpose being to defend the island from invaders and protect this key shipping port from the English and the French.

Ironically, the fortification system, constructed from giant blocks of granite, was based on a French design. It incorporated parapets and brick vaults to provide secure enclosures for the men - plus an inner fort surrounded by a deep and wide dry moat.

The theory being that anyone that had the balls to build such a formidable fortress would be a very tough opponent indeed, and put off anyone thinking of invading.

But the project was as ambitious as it was hard to realise. And, as one elaborate design was scrapped in favour of another, the whole thing kept getting stopped and restarted. As time passed and new people with new ideas took control of the project, the cost became untenable, and the Fort was never really finished. At least not before its original purpose become quite redundant.

The world changed. The wars never came. No invading flotilla hove into view, and no cannon was ever fired in battle.

Today, La Mola is a mere remnant of its former glory and is no longer a working military base. But it remains a magnificent tribute to engineering, vision, monumentally bad political judgement, and sheer bloody mindedness.

On the plus side, the Fortress now serves as a key Menorcan tourist attraction, seeing many thousands of visitors a year. Parts of it are also rented out for social events such as Weddings and Parties.

Some of the original structure is for external viewing only and closed to the public. Tours are accompanied and viewing times are restricted.

So, it was odd that on this dark and windy evening someone was atop the eastern-most tower overlooking the harbour.

From this vantage point a person had a clear line of sight directly across to the other side of the harbour channel.

In bygone days this high perch also gave the original Vickers Armstrong gun operators a clean 360 sweep of the sea area around the mouth of the Harbour. The sentry would be able to guard the channel from any approaching enemy ships and fire warning shots with the mighty cannon that was once installed here. Sadly, all that remained now was its crumbling circular base.

But now someone was using this as a base to use a more modern and deadly weapon - a high-powered assault rifle with built-in silencer. They were kneeling with the stock hugged tight into their shoulder, looking through its telescopic night-site, tracing it along the Es Castell and Calas Fonts areas on the other side of the harbour.

A small adjustment on the scope and the scene across the water swam sharply into the rifleman's view.

As always at this time of the evening Calas Fonts was busy. The waterside area is given over almost exclusively to restaurants, bars and shops. It is a favourite haunt of those that want some decent food in a lively atmosphere, or just fancy some evening retail therapy.

The rifleman stopped tracking the scene and focussed the site on someone putting out an awning in front of a small leather goods shop. Though it was quite dark now, the infrared made everything easy to see.

Moving along once more: a traffic warden was ticketing a parked van: a young woman passed by on a moped: there was an old couple walking their dogs. The masts of yachts moored along the harbour bobbed up occasionally into view in front of these goings on.

Nothing unusual to see. But that was the point. It was a typical evening in Calas Fonts. People generally milled around, stopping to browse in the shop windows or study the menus, chatting with friends sat at tables outside of the many restaurants that ran the entire length of the area.

A woman appeared from a doorway carrying a shopping bag. The rifle site followed her until she stopped to look in a shop window. The gunman made an adjustment to the focus until the crosshairs were pin sharp across her back.

Yes. She would do nicely. The shooter exhaled slowly, calmed himself and slowly squeezed the trigger.

The rifle stock jerked slightly. The woman's head went down suddenly, followed by the rest of her.

'What the …?' There were no bullets in the gun! This was merely a practice. A dry run.

Panic began to set in. Sweating despite the chill evening air, the shooter felt glued to the spot, unable to stop watching the surreal scene unfolding through the scope.

Then all became clear.

The woman stood up from having bent down to retrieve her reading glasses from where she had dropped them on the ground.

The shooter smiled. Greatly relieved. You couldn't make it up!

Yet it proved one thing. Maybe this was not the best way to get the job done. Yes, the view was good, but that alone could not be relied upon. From this distance the shot would be hard enough to make. There were just too many variables – people walking in front of the target, bobbing masts getting in the way, a strong crosswind - there were just too many things that could go wrong.

On the day of the deed there would be more people, more

boats with masts, more everything. And, considering the importance of the target and security around them, there would only be time for one shot.

And what if they decided to locate the target elsewhere, further into the port? The distance would make an accurate shot almost impossible.

No. There had to be a better way. Something that could not fail to eliminate the victim.

The shooter put down the rifle, lit a cigarette, then began mulling over the options until interrupted by the sudden screeching of some gulls heading down the channel.

It gave the gunman an idea.

AT THE AMERICAN BAR

It was frustrating. Three weeks investigating the untimely and bizarre death of Mayor Alfonso but Inspector Juan and his team were no nearer to establishing if this was an accident - a prank gone wrong, or a deliberate murder.

All those that had participated in the Slaughter of The Rag Dolls had been questioned repeatedly. But none had admitted kidnapping the Mayor or planning to kill him.

Every one of their weapons had been checked and tested but none had proven to have been firing live ammo. There were no fingerprints or DNA trace that could link any of them to the victim.

So, after 3 weeks of intense investigation, Menorca's finest had, ironically, drawn a blank. No confession, no evidence, no clues that would lead them to the perpetrator of this deed – be it an accident or otherwise.

As he pulled into his parking bay at Mahon Police

Headquarters, Juan was dreading reporting his lack of findings to his boss.

He knew she already had a low opinion of him. Now, this would ensure that he would be back down in the basement, wading through the X, Y and Z files once more.

Not that he felt it was his fault. Many cases went this way until there was a break. He just needed a bit more time. But without some sort of lead, or divine intervention, it looked like he was heading back down below.

He started rehearsing his arguments as he rode up in the lift to face his boss in her lair, as he considered it. By the time he left again an hour later, he was beside himself with anger, her sarcastic comments still ringing in his ears.

'Call yourself a Detective!' 'This should have been an open and shut case.' 'Three weeks and you've got absolutely nothing!' 'I think the basement may be the best place for you after all.'

He'd tried to argue that there was so little evidence in this case it was hard to know yet if it was an accident or murder, and basically, he could find the truth if he had more time.

'More time? Hah!' She looked at him with cold contempt, then at the wall calendar behind her office door. He felt sure he was about to be taken off the case.

She saw his pained expression and then sighed shaking her head and said 'Right. I'll give you one more week.'

At this Juan brightened. She quickly dampened his spirits again saying 'Only because you have done so well in the past. But don't think your former glory is going to cut any ice with me. I want results this time.'

'One week and that's it. If you haven't cracked it by then...' She let the sentence hang and simply looked purposefully down through the floor.

He left the building in a funk. How dare she talk to him like that. Like some junior who had spilled coffee on her copy of *Guns and Ammo* or knocked over one of the nasty little Cactus plants that sat on her desk.

Well nuts to that! He was a good detective. He was going to show her just how good by cracking this case. He just needed a break. A bit of a helping hand.

He knew his boss would not officially agree to it, but that was no reason to rule it out. He would call Frank Harmer. If anyone could help him get to the bottom of this one it was Frank. He called him on his mobile.

Frank sounded happy and too not surprised to hear from him. It was almost as if he was expecting Juan to call.

They exchanged pleasantries and without going into detail arranged to meet at lunchtime in the American Bar - a short walk from police HQ. Frank already had a good idea what it was all about and was delighted to be considered once more for his considerable expertise.

Besides, he was getting bored now that Marisol was not around and was looking forward to having a good chinwag with his police chum, as well as having his brains picked about a tricky crime.

He was already sat at one of the tables, at the rear of the café when Juan arrived.

The establishment was done out like a classic 50's American diner. There was a long bar with a brass handrail wrapped around it, with the other two thirds of the room given over to dining tables. Black and white and sepia pictures of the American Bar in bygone eras adorned the walls.

The smell of cigarette smoke and over-roasted coffee beans were a permanent fixture. But it was a price you had to pay if you wanted to have a discreet meeting and private conversation, away from the outside dining area where most people tended to congregate.

As he was not officially engaged on this case, Frank knew that Juan would want to have this meeting on the QT.

Walking in from the bright midday sunshine, it took a few moments for Juan's eyes to adjust and spot his police consultant friend.

No one came to show him to a table and take his order. The staff were too busy serving lunches to customers at the tables outside to notice this new customer.

Luckily, Frank had already been served and had a pot of coffee and some pastries waiting.

The two men shook hands warmly and Juan sat down with his back to the door. He did not want news of this meeting to reach the ears of Chief Volterra and give her any more reasons to think he could not crack this case on his own.

Besides, all he was doing was having coffee with his friend, who just happened to be an excellent detective with an international reputation for solving difficult and high-profile crimes.

'Señor Harmer. So good to see you again. You look very well.'

This made Frank laugh. 'I'm just glad to get out of the house. Been going stir crazy. And you? You are well?'

Juan nodded but it wasn't convincing.

Frank said 'You look…concerned.' Pretending to be a psychotherapist taking notes, he said in his best Sigmund Freud impression 'Tell me young fellow, vot zeems to be ze problem?'

The attempt at humour was lost on the policeman. He drummed his fingers on the tabletop, shook his head and said 'It is this damn case. It's baffling. I am getting nowhere with it. I thought I should run it by you. See what you think.'

Frank smiled and nodded but felt there was something more that was troubling his friend. He said 'Sure. No problem. But I get the impression there is something else that is driving you around the bend.'

Juan looked confused. 'What? Well I have my car, but. I don't see what…'

Frank's sudden laughter made him realise that it was an English idiom and he got the gist. 'Ah. Yes. I see.' With a sigh he added 'It's my new boss!'

'Oh dear. Bit of a hard arse is he?'

Juan reached in his jacket for a fresh pack of cigarettes. He unwrapped the cellophane and screwed it into a tight ball. Throwing it angrily to one side he said 'Yes. She is. A *pain* in the ass to be exact.'

For the next thirty minutes he unburdened himself about this new source of vexation in his life.

He realised when Frank excused himself for a trip to the loo that he hadn't yet mentioned the Mayor murder case.

So, on Frank's return he filled him in on all the details. He told him how frustrating and difficult it was having such a lack of clues, and that he had just one more week to get results.

Did Frank have any insights or ideas?

The ex-detective sat back and rubbed his jaw. 'Well, there are some interesting aspects to consider. It is a difficult one for sure. Let me think about it for a while and get back to you.'

Frank waved to the waiter who was now back behind the bar and mouthed the words 'la cuenta' making a hand gesture of signing something as he did so.

As the man approached, Juan took out a 20 Euro note and dropped it onto the table. Frank went to argue and reached for his own wallet, but Juan held up his hand and said. 'No. My treat. I will get this.'

As they stood outside the American Bar saying goodbye, Juan laid his hand on Frank's arm and said 'Thank you for meeting me here today. I really appreciate it my friend. Anything you can come up with will be greatly received. I shall consider it a big favour'

He felt a little bad that he was taking advantage of their friendship and added 'I wish I could bring you in on this

case as an official consultant. But this new boss is just…
well, we would have to prove there has been foul play.
Then we could get the case elevated.'

He smiled half-heartedly. 'But I think for that I will need a
bit of luck. Some new development that would blow this
case wide open.'

Luckily, though neither man could have anticipated how,
that very thing was about to happen.

LA FIESTA DE SANT JOAN. 'DEAD RINGER'

Somewhere in the dark shadows of the warm summer stable a lone figure crouches. The horses, sensing this presence, whinny and shuffle nervously. It is a scent they do not recognise, but they are highly trained and they do not panic as he stealthily moves among them.

The interloper hears the sound of people approaching and quickly slips back into the dark shadows.

The Fiesta of Saint Joan in June is a very big deal in Ciutadella.

There is much preparation. Children look forward with an excitement second only to Christmas. Teenagers consider it an opportunity to flirt, drink and hang with their friends. Working adults are grateful for the extended holiday.
At the heart of every Menorcan Fiesta is the *Jaleo* or 'horse dance'. It is a Menorcan festive ritual that goes back to the beginning of the fourteenth century.

Magnificent large black Menorcan horses are adorned with ribbons, embroideries and multi-coloured carnations. Their riders, known as Caxiers, are dressed in traditional smart black uniforms from the days when the British Navy ruled the waves, and the roost in Menorca.

With their coat-tailed jackets trimmed with gold braid, tricorn hats, white breeches and long leather riding boots, they are a spectacular sight to see as they parade along the town streets, and perform traditional games of horsemanship in the village squares.

The Caixers show off their horse mastery skills to music, making their mounts perform elegant and dexterous movements that require the highest level of training and horsemanship knowledge.

This is clearly demonstrated when, to shouts of encouragement from the crowd, the Caixers not only get their horses to rear-up in a calm and controlled fashion, but also to walk along on their hind legs!

The parts of town where the parades and games take place are cordoned off from traffic with barriers. Sawdust is spread thickly all over the streets to stop the horses from sliding. Many shops shut but some bars and cafés stay open.

The Fiesta of Saint Joan starts on a Sunday with the traditional handing over of the flag of Sant Joan by the Caixer Senyor (Senior Rider and President) to the Caixer Fadri - an unmarried rider whose responsibility it is to carry the flag throughout the fiesta. This is followed by the presentation of a live Ram, paraded on the shoulders of a barefooted young man (for some obscure reason), and then later the Jaleo, and a series of Medieval style tourney games on horseback.

Today is Monday and the Fiesta de Sant Joan de Ciutadella is in full swing.

It's a hot one, and people are out in their shorts and sun hats. The town centre is packed. Lively music blares from loudspeakers hung amid the myriad reams of bunting adorning the telephone wires and lamp posts.

Miguel Ferragut has shut his shoe shop for the day. He stands outside it and looks at his watch. He turns to his wife and says testily 'They are late starting again this year!'

His wife frowns at him. 'Will you relax and stop clock watching. It is Fiesta time. Which is also stop clock-watching time.'

He shrugs and says 'Well I am just saying. I shut up shop early. So, I have lost sales. Precious customers. You would think they could start things on time!'

His wife looks at him and laughs. 'Hah. You think they organise all this just for you? Of course, they say 'be quick' Miguel Ferragut is waiting. There will be hell to pay if we start late!'

Miguel knits his brow, trying to come up with a pithy retort, when the tinny music blaring through the speakers changes suddenly from pop music to a traditional Military March.

Now he brightens and rubs his hands together. Here comes the parade of the Caixers! Everyone applauds enthusiastically and there is a movement through the crowd like a ripple towards the head of the street.

Horses and riders approach at a slow trot in ones and twos,

their magnificent stallions prancing and snorting. Sweat and foam coating their bodies in the mid-day heat.

The crowd yells and cheers and blows horns. This makes the horses edgy and excited, but none will panic or bolt as they are highly trained and in the firm control of their riders.

The cavalcade proceeds to the Plaça des Born and the 'Jaleo' takes place. The huge horses rear up in turn as each rider tries to get their horse to walk the furthest distance on its hind legs.

The cheers get louder with each performance. More Pomada is drunk.

Of course, there is an element of risk that one of the horses may bolt or simply crash down onto someone in the crowd. Especially as it is customary to try and touch the horse's heart for good luck when it is rearing up.

The public are just a few feet from the prancing horses which, being of a very large breed, weigh the best part of half a ton each in full regalia with rider atop, and there have been a few serious accidents in the past.

Today there will be no such tragedies. But there will be a fatality at the Fiesta de Sant Joan.

As the afternoon progresses, we reach one of the highlights, and perhaps the most dangerous part of the proceedings. The 's'Ensortilla'. Here the most accomplished and daring riders compete against one another. Each is armed with a long metal lance and attempts to spear a suspended ring onto its tip at full gallop.

As the crowd is so close and the lances so sharp, there is always the potential for a serious mishap. Which is why all riders must carry their lance aloft and slanting upwards in front of them, to ensure they only spear the ring, not another rider or a bystander.

Now a buzz goes around the crowd. Who will secure the ring? *Ortega!* Everyone knows he is the best. Ortega will spear the ring on first pass, as always. Ortega the brave. Ortega the bold.

aka Ortega the handsome.

For, as well as a fine horseman, he has quite the reputation as a '*Don Juan*'. And there have been many rumours of his amorous dalliances with certain single women (and quite a few married ones).

When Ortega rides by, the children will wave flags. The men will clap or jeer. Women will blow kisses and throw flowers.

Now the first rider comes. There are rousing cheers and then disappointed sighs. It is not Ortega. The hoof beats pound as the mighty steed hurtles by just inches from the crowd. You can feel the rush of air and flecks of spume as it passes. You can smell the sweat as it mingles in the air with the clouds of sawdust kicked up.

It is Alonso Sanchez and he charges at the hanging prize. The sun is glinting off the chest-high lance shaft. He thrusts. He misses the ring. The crowd lets out cries of anguish. He gallops on and disappears around the end of the street.

A chant starts 'Ortega! Ortega!' The second horse and rider thunder out and down the human gauntlet of waving and cheering (and slightly drunk) townsfolk.

It fades away as it is another rider, not Ortega. The new man charges and raises his lance, tilting at the small silver ring hanging by a thin thread overhead. He too misses the prize and the crowd mumbles its disappointment.

Now there is a tangible silence of anticipation. There is only more one rider to come. Surely, it must be Ortega. The hoof beats approach from around the end of the street. The horse and rider power into view.

The crowd recognizes his red plumed hat and ceremonial sash – the one that is only worn by the premier Caixer. The best horseman on the island.

Ortega!

The crowd goes wild. But their shouts of triumph soon turn to cries of shock and confusion, as it is clear something is wrong with Ortega.

As the horse gallops forward, we can see that the rider is angled strangely. Not sitting proudly upright but lazily forward. He arches backward as the horse gathers pace. A glint of sunlight catches the steel lance that is pointing upwards as he holds it at his chest.

But wait. He is not just holding it. It looks almost as if he is trying to pull it from his chest! There are screams as people realise that is just what he is doing. With sickening horror they can now see that the lance is stuck right through him!

His face is a mask of terror and pain. Blood runs from the edges of his open mouth. He clutches desperately at the spear in a futile attempt to dislodge it. The horse gallops on oblivious to the predicament of its master.

As Ortega enters the 's'Ensortilla' arena, his dying body slides from the saddle and onto the ground. The crowd can only watch and is frozen in fear. He twitches. He gasps, still clutching the spear to his chest, blood oozing through his fingers. He tries to speak. Then he slumps lifeless, his arms falling like weights to his sides.

His lifeblood pooling in the sawdust.

DI Juan looked down at the body and shook his head. What the hell? How?

He was deep in thought and did not notice Frank Harmer arriving. The sound of his voice made him start.

'Shocking business.' Frank looked around at the now deserted square. The empty beer cans and water bottles. The track of disturbed sawdust where the horses had charged in for the contest. The hanging buntings flapping lazily in the breeze. Crime scene tapes sectioning off and preventing entry into the area.

Somewhere nearby the Fiesta had resumed, and the sound of music carried to them on the breeze. The cheers and applause of the crowd were somewhat muted in comparison to several hours earlier, before the 'tragedy' happened.

The forensic team was finishing up. Little red and green markers had been placed on the ground where splashes of blood and other debris had been found.

The scene was grim. The deceased Caixer lay on his side, blood pooled on the ground beneath his hunched form. A long silver-grey metal lance ran through his body front-to-back, like a shish kebab skewer. The rider's saddle and hat had been placed neatly on the ground beside him as if in respect.

'Such a shame.' Detective Juan's voice was little more than a whisper. Frank could have sworn the man was close to tears. He gave Juan a sympathetic but questioning look. Juan smiled suddenly and simply said 'Ortega.'

'Or - what?'

'This is - or was Ortega. The bravest and the best Caixer ever to have worn the sash.'

'Oh, I see.' Frank nodded and bent to look more closely at the victim. After a few seconds he stood up straight and asked. 'So why would someone want to kill him?'

Detective Juan shrugged. 'Well, it looks that way, but how can we be sure this wasn't some kind of freak accident?'

Frank shook his head slowly. 'It's not what the evidence is saying. See here...' With his walking stick he pointed at the end of the lance, stained in bloody fingerprints. 'This lance was driven through the victim's breastbone. It pierced his heart and then went right through. Must have taken some force to do that.'

Juan agreed 'Sure. But it still could be an accident.'

Frank continued 'Then there's the angle the lance entered the body.'

Juan raised his eyebrows in question.

'A Caixer holds his lance like this when charging.' He demonstrated with his walking stick, placing it near his midriff and pointing straight out in front of him. He also bent forward slightly as if on horseback and charging, his left hand holding the imaginary reins.

'So, if it *was* an accident and he ran into something solid that pushed the lance into him, it's unlikely that it would have entered at such an extreme angle. What's more, why was he holding the lance the wrong way round? Sharp end toward him?'

'What?' Juan checked and saw that frank was right. He whistled and scratched his head as Frank continued. 'No Caixer would have made that mistake.'

He stroked his chin and said with certainty 'No. Someone murdered our friend here.'

Juan couldn't argue with this logic but was still puzzled. 'Okay. But why would anyone want to kill Ortega? What would be the motive?'

Frank looked down at the body once more and, careful not to contaminate the crime scene, he examined the hat and saddle. He turned the saddle over and from beneath removed a post-it note that had been stuck there.

'Ah. I thought so.'

There was something drawn on it. He held it up so that the policeman could see and said 'I think we might have found the answer to that.'

Juan had a sharp intake of breath. In what looked like red lipstick was a heart symbol with an arrow through it.

Beneath this was written the number 7.

SLEEPLESS IN MADRID

It was late and Frank was tired.

Still, the Skype connection was good. He sat on the edge of the bed with his laptop open. A glass of scotch untouched on the bedside table.

Marisol's face appeared on the screen. He thought she looked a bit down, so he tried to keep the mood light and cheerful. 'Hi. How are things there in sunny old Madrid?'

Frank wasn't a huge fan of Madrid. He didn't like big cities. In fact, he thought Madrid was one of the nicer ones, but it had rained non-stop for 3 of the 5 days of the site-seeing trip he had been on with his late wife Linda.

However, he *was* a big fan of one of Madrid's most famous landmarks - Atocha Railway Station, where they spent many afternoons in its dry and delightful surroundings. The first ever built in Madrid in 1851, the building is a masterpiece of construction in wrought iron and glass. Its vast arched end window consists of rising vertical mosaic panels, held in a crisscrossing lattice of intricately woven metalwork.

Its cavernous concourse features subtropical gardens laid out in a series of leafy avenues, along which visitors can wander in wonder at the huge variety of succulents and plants.

These are all kept in warm nurturing conditions by an ingenious system of pipes venting gentle clouds of warm mist at frequent intervals, much to the surprise and delight of visitors.

There is an open café area where visitors can relax between journeys, taking in the exotic greenery, arty sculptures, and the charming activities of the terrapins living and breeding happily in man-made lily ponds.

This was the one and only reason Frank could ever contemplate returning to Spain's capital city again. Of course, it was different for Marisol. Madrid was where she grew up and where most of her family including her own grown-up children lived. But now she was there it seemed a million miles away.

Marisol rolled her eyes and said 'It is very hot here. It's not easy to sleep at night. How are things with you?'

He thought he wouldn't mention the murder case and just said 'Oh, y'know. Same old.'

He didn't want to pry, but felt he had to ask 'How's it all going with your situation over there? Any chance you'll be returning to Menorca soon?'

Marisol managed a half smile and said 'It's not going as well as I had hoped. Not at all in fact.'

Frank could see that this was upsetting to her and said 'Oh dear. Well, I've been watering your plants and feeding your tropical fish. They told me they are missing you and can't wait for you to be home.'

This did not get the reaction he was hoping for. She looked away and upwards as if searching for something off in the corner of the room, then forced another smile as she said.

'Things could be going better here. I think it's going to take a while to sort this matter out.'

He was dying to ask for details, but it seemed that the 'matter' was very personal and that she didn't want to, or couldn't, share any of it with him.

He simply said 'Oh. I see. That's a shame.'

They were silent for a while. She seemed wrapped in her thoughts. He saw tears welling in her eyes.

He knew he should say something and blurted out 'So do you think you will be much longer?'

Idiot! Could he have said anything more crass?

What he really wanted to say was that he was missing her. A lot. But that was clearly going to make things worse too. Best to say something more cheery and non-contentious and end on a positive note. Let her get some rest.

Yes. After she had sorted out this business whatever it was, they could pick up where they left off when she returned home to Menorca.

Then the bad news came. She took a deep breath, but it came out in little more than a whisper. 'I might have to… stay.'

'Huh? What? A little bit longer? Oh, that's a shame. But I guess if you have to then you…'

She interrupted. 'No. I mean I have to *stay*. A lot longer. Perhaps a very long time. Maybe… for good. I don't know.' A sadness filled her eyes. She looked away so that she didn't have to meet his gaze.

She bit her lip. Went to say something else then stopped.

For a few moments they just sat and stared at each other. Thoughts tumbled and words jangled like fragments of broken glass through their minds. Words that they wanted to say. Feelings yet unspoken.

The silence was broken only by the chirruping of crickets floating in on the night air through the open window.

It was Frank that finally spoke. 'Look. It's very late and you and I both need to get some sleep.' He gave her a reassuring smile and added 'I'm sure it won't look so bad in the morning.'

He resisted the impulse to blow her a kiss. It seemed inappropriate somehow. 'Talk again soon.'

She gave him a tearful smile. The Skype screen winked off with a jolly popping sound.

FIESTA DE SANT ANTONI 'DEAD HEAD'

The town of Fornells lies in the north East of Menorca. Situated at the mouth of a wide and shallow bay, it is popular with sail enthusiasts. In fact, there are windsurfing and sailing schools sited all along the road that skirts the bay and leads into the town.

Fornells is small and mainly residential with a few main streets. It has a pretty harbour walk, a small esplanade featuring cafés and tourist shops, and some historic military structures situated on the quayside at the far end of the town.

The town's buildings are a mix of Menorcan architectures. They feature everything from villas with neat gardens to luxury apartment blocks that occupy the seafront area. The back streets are more traditional with old-fashioned Menorcan terraces and small local business premises.

Every 4th weekend in July, Fornells sees the annual festival of Sant Antoni. It kicks off, as Menorcan Fiestas do, with the ringing of the bells and a piper playing. These are followed by the parade of local marching bands and the *els gegants i capgrossos*, the giants with the big heads!

These comical characters feature in most Menorcan Fiestas and are eagerly looked forward to with glee by adults and children alike.

The giant 'Puppets' are expertly constructed by local people to represent traditional Menorcan peasant men and women, and prominent historic and present day Menorcans.

These large caricature figures, with long cloth bodies and giant heads, are often fashioned to look like local dignitaries or well-known local bigwigs. The grotesque facsimiles often have unflattering exaggerated facial features - overbites, bushy eyebrows, puffed up lips, big noses - clearly designed to ridicule the person on whom each Giant figure is fashioned.

Every year, the old characters and the new 'victims' make everyone roar with laughter at their inaugural appearance.

This year, one of the giant heads has been fashioned to look like Angelica Starr. A local celebrity and once famous pop star with a string of international hits.

In her 70's heyday, her name was linked to pop bad boys such as Mick Jagger. Now in retirement in her gated villa, she is often in the local papers because of her lavish and lively all-night parties, that almost always draw complaints from her neighbours.

With so many stories of her sordid goings on, it is no wonder that today we are seeing her portrayed in larger than life papier-mache and paraded along the streets of this town.

These clever constructions are operated from the inside by strong individuals strapped into a kind of shoulder harness. Occupants of the tall ones have to master the skill of walking on stilts, as they weave their dancing way through the packed town streets at the head of the parade.

Today it is hot inside the Giant Heads. Much water is being consumed by the costume wearers. Dancing in an outfit that weighs some 100 lbs, in 30 degrees of heat requires you to be very fit. It also takes a lot of practice as, with just a discreet viewing slit, it is not easy to see where you are going.

The pop queen's caricature is instantly recognized and draws loud peals of laughter from the crowds as soon as it makes its entrance. 'Look! It's Angelica Starr!'

The people laugh even louder as the grotesque look-alike weaves comically about the street, almost colliding with a lamp post and then lurching back into the lineup of the parade to join its fellows.

The performer who is now walking around wearing her Giant Head is obviously milking their part.

As the music grows in tempo and the parade advances along the harbour road, so 'Angelica Starr's' dancing becomes more and more erratic. She walks into a tree. Then she stumbles into the crowd, who promptly right her and push her back into the parade. Finally, she stops, lurches backwards, falls to the ground, rolls around and then lies very still.

The Giant Head lolls about as the rest of the parade passes. The occupant's body is hanging out from the waist down.

After a few moments, when it becomes clear that the figure is not about to rise again, several people run forward from the crowd. Pedro Alvarez kneels down to look inside. People piloting the Gigantes sometimes faint from the effort on hot days. So, it would be a good idea to extricate this unfortunate person from the structure, get them to the roadside, and administer some cold water.

Pedro can see by the shape of the legs that the occupant is a woman, and that she is clearly tangled in the support straps of the giant head. This will require more help.

He calls to a friend in the watching crowd, where giggles of mirth have turned to murmurs of concern, as they can see that the unfortunate occupant is not moving at all.

'Fernando! Give us a hand here for heaven's sake. She is a dead weight you know!'

Fernando Florit comes over, examines the prone figure and says 'Yes. I think she is also dead drunk, judging by the smell of Gin.'

Pedro hasn't really noticed this, having consumed quite a bit of Pomada himself, but now agrees she does smell strongly of alcohol. But it does not seem to Pedro that she smells of Gin only. There is something else. Something familiar that he can't quite place.

They untangle her from the support straps and gently extricate her from her Head 'cage'. Carrying her between them to the kerb, they can see she is not in a good state. Her hair is wrapped around her face and stuck to it with sweat. Her eyes, what they can see of them, are unfocussed. What looks like orange froth is trickling from the sides of her mouth as her head lolls from side-to-side as they move her.

They set her down at the roadside. Her arms lie loosely by her sides. Her legs awkwardly akimbo. There is no sign of her breathing. No sound comes from her at all.

Pedro reaches down and gently removes the hair from her face. To his horror, and to the assembled crowd, he quickly realises who she is. 'Oh my saints!' Cries a woman. 'It's her! Angelica Starr!'

'Yes, look!' Shouts another. They all look on in disbelief. They glance back to the empty giant head revolving slowly in the street. In her present disheveled state, she looks surprisingly like her exaggerated papier-mache representation.

They look at her once more, this time more carefully. Surely not! It can't be, can it? But yes, it is. Angelica Starr, former pop princess and local party girl lies on the ground before them.

Not dead drunk. Just dead.

Frank Harmer hated mortuaries.

It wasn't the bodies. He was used to that. It was the smell. Death and chemicals. It was a smell that seemed to be unique to forensic labs. And on this very warm and close day that smell seemed to be overpowering.

In fact, the lab was air-conditioned and the temperature and humidity very comfortable. But he still felt nauseous from the moment he entered.

Inspector Juan was stood next to a table on which lay a body partly covered in a blue plastic sheet. He was talking with the pathologist on duty. Dr Garcia.

They stopped and turned toward him as he approached. Juan was first to speak. His face lit up and with a beaming smile he said 'Ah. Here is the man that will have all the answers!' Then with a mock dramatic gesture 'Carlos, I present to you Detective Inspector Francis Harmer of the London Metropolitan Police.'

The Pathologist held out a bloodstained gloved hand, which Frank promptly ignored. He simply nodded and smiled at the man.

The police surgeon cleared his throat and said politely 'Ah yes. The famous master detective who can solve any crime with a click of his fingers!' He winked and attempted to snap his fingers, but the gore covered rubber glove simply squeaked.

Even though this was meant in friendly jest, Frank felt embarrassed. There followed an awkward silence. Frank was first to speak.

'So...' He gestured at the corpse. '...another one? I assume that's why you asked me down here.'

Juan nodded and then asked the pathologist to show his findings. The man in the coveralls pulled back the sheet to reveal the naked corpse of former international pop singer Angelica Starr.

It was an unsettling sight.

True, she no longer looked disheveled. She had been washed, her hair brushed, and her eyes closed so that she looked almost peaceful. But the large black stitches from the recent autopsy, that now seemed to hold the two halves of her chest and abdomen together, looked so incongruous. An insult that was always a jolt to Frank's sensibilities every time he saw it on a murder victim.

He thought back to all the deceased crime victims he had seen this way, *'filleted and stitched and lying on a cold slab like some gutted…'*

'I already know who killed this woman!' The Pathologist's sudden declaration made him jump.

The two lawmen gave him a questioning look. He paused and looked at them with a serious expression, then announced triumphantly 'It was… *The Don*!'

Then he and Juan broke into fits of laughter, like two schoolboys sharing a silly joke.

It took several moments for Frank to work it out. Then he remembered the branded *'Don Drenaje'* cleaning product from those cheesy TV commercials. He didn't see the funny side.

He gave them both an old-fashioned look and then asked 'Drain Cleaning Fluid? Is that what you are saying killed her?'

The Pathologist sensed that his morgue humour might seem out of place to those that didn't do this for a living. He did not want to appear unprofessional to the 'Great' Detective, and he became serious again.

'Sorry, just a little path lab humour.' 'Yes.' He walked over to a shelf and brought back a jar half filled with an orangey brown liquid. 'We found this in her estómago, her stomach.'

He held it out for Frank to smell, who gagged as soon as he did so. 'Strewth! That's quite a cocktail!'

The Pathologist held the jar up to the light and studied it as if it were a glass of fine wine. 'Drain Cleaner. Gin. Rohypnol. Bile. Various food particles and...' He held it to his nose and sniffed. 'A hint of garlic!'

Here he laughed merrily once more, thinking they would appreciate this new joke.

No? Tough morgue.

Frank looked at Juan and said 'Well I am sure you wouldn't down that lot on purpose. So, we are looking at a possible murder, yes? Any number?'

Juan furrowed his brow, then realised what Frank was asking. He became quite excited. 'Ah! At first, I did not think so. No piece of paper secreted on her. No note in any body cavity.' He winced at the memory of his boss taunting him.

The Path man shook his head in confirmation.

'But then…' He reached down and gently lifted the dead woman's right ear '…we found this!' Behind her ear, drawn in what appeared to be purple permanent marker they could clearly see the number 6.

Frank was puzzled. 'Six?' This didn't seem to fit the theory he was now working on, that all the numbers they had found on the victims corresponded to the Ten Commandments in the Holy Bible.

He had run his theory by Juan who had agreed it was a

possibility.

However, this one didn't seem to fit the pattern.

He scratched his head. 'The sixth commandment is 'thou shalt not kill' isn't it? How does it apply in this case? Did she ever kill anyone?'

Juan looked at him. Raised an eyebrow and said. 'Perhaps your 'Ten Commandments' theory is wrong my friend and the numbers mean something else.'

Frank thought about this for a moment. Of course, he could be wrong. But he had a gut feeling that he was on the right track. Then he remembered something he had seen in the papers a while back. 'What about that crash? When she was DUI? Driving Under the Influence? Were there any casualties?'

'Oh yes. I remember.' Juan tried to recall the details. It was before his time in the Menorca police, but he had just read the report as background for this investigation.

'She hit a statue on the middle of a roundabout near the airport late at night. She tried to drive off again on the wrong side of the road and drove into the path of a taxi which ended up in a drainage ditch.'

'Was anyone in the taxi? Any passengers I mean?'

'An old couple just coming back from a wedding. They weren't hurt, just badly shaken. Wait a minute...I believe the old fellow died a few weeks later. His wife blamed the shock of the incident, but they could not prove anything.'

'And Angelica Starr. What did she get?'

'She got a caution and was made to pay for the repair of the Taxi.' Here Juan grinned and shook his head. 'Also, the restoration of the statue.'

'So, no one blamed her for the death of the Taxi passenger then? No-one except the poor man's wife that is.'

Juan pursed his lips and shook his head. Then the Path Man piped up. 'I remember that one. I had him in here, of course. It was Abelardo Rubio from Mijgorn. A very popular old man. Family restaurant business. Would have reached his 90th Birthday if he hadn't died. Big funeral. Nice food.'

Now it began to make sense after all. *Thou shalt not kill.* Frank was more certain than ever. They had a serial killer on their hands.

If he was right, there would be a familiar figure in the crowd of the Fiesta of St Antoni on the day that the latest victim was murdered.

'CCTV?' He asked.

'There were two cameras in that street. And we have some footage from around the area for the 24 hours before. Shops, car parks, petrol stations and such. Our guys are checking through it right now.'

'Then let's go take a look.'

'THE WORD OF GOD'

Juan closed the Venetian blinds that covered the large window, just enough to shield them from the glare of the evening sun.

It was warm in the room and the sunlight would also make it difficult to see the whiteboard that filled most of the back wall. This was a crime scene chart and was divided into three sections with titles - *April: Easter Shooting.* - *June: St Joan Fiesta Murder* - *July: Fornells Fiesta Murder.* Each section was dotted with photos, clues and notes written in felt tip marker.

The assembled officers, about a dozen in all, sat at desks lined up in rows facing the 'Crime Line' chart.

To Frank, it felt like being back in a school classroom. Or worse, back at a Met briefing.

Inspector Juan stood in front of the board, quietly studying the crime collage. He then turned to face the room like a teacher preparing to introduce today's lesson to the class.

He spoke in English, mainly for the benefit of Frank. 'It would seem that we are not dealing with three separate murders here. But we may be dealing with…' He paused for dramatic effect 'a serial killer!' He looked around at the assembled faces. They registered shock and disbelief. A serial killer! Here in little old Menorca!

He let that sink in for a moment and then went on. 'How do we know this? What gives us reason to make this deduction?' Here he nodded briefly in the direction of Frank. 'Well, there is a pattern emerging that tells us so.'

He turned back to the board and pointed at the pieces of numbered paper that had been found on each of the victims. They were sealed in plastic zip-lock evidence bags and stuck to the board at each event.

'Yes. It may seem obvious now. But my esteemed friend and valued police consultant Señor Frank Harmer has been very helpful in establishing this.' He nodded at Frank, who by now really needed no introduction to police officers in Menorca.

His involvement in helping them crack the murder case of a retired Banker, whose body turned up in Binibeca Bay, and the bringing down of a major smuggling ring was the stuff of legend among the Menorca police fraternity.

Frank blushed and nodded slightly in acknowledgement.

Juan continued 'He has a theory which I am sure he will now be happy to share with you.' He suddenly looked at them all and sternly said. 'Take notes please as I will be asking questions later!' There was a silence followed by nervous laughter as Juan broke into a huge grin and said. 'Just kidding!'

'Señor Harmer. If you would be so kind.' He sat down on a chair to one side and gave the floor to Frank.

Señor Harmer was nervous. It had been a while since he had given any kind of briefing and was surprised at just how hot and sweaty he was. He took off his jacket and hung it near the door.

He eyed them all slowly, then said 'I found the answer in the Bible.'

They looked bewildered. What did he say? The Bible? Was he talking about the crimes or had he found religion?

They looked around at one another, eyebrows raised. Ah, this was probably another joke. The English sense of humour.

But no. They could see that Frank was serious. He continued 'From the start, the first victim, that was clearly a murder.' He tapped the board below the picture of the dead mayor in the Rag Doll get-up at the first crime scene. 'Live rounds were used. Three shots. Here, here and here. He pointed to the diagram of a body where the shots were indicted. 'Then there was this…' He flicked the piece of paper bearing the number 8. 'This had been placed in the victim's mouth.'

'Clearly, someone was sending us a message.' He looked at the blank faces. 'Any idea what that message was?' They gave each other questioning looks, then one hand went up tentatively.

Officer Maria Delgado offered 'You said the answer was in the Bible. Does the number refer to a verse or passage perhaps?'

Frank gave her an encouraging smile and said. 'Yes. You are not a million miles away.' He could see she wasn't sure what he meant.

'What I mean is, I think you are correct. Almost.'

Officer Delgado returned an appreciative smile.

Another, Officer Mateo Sintes spoke up, but he was playing to the crowd. 'Perhaps it was the avenging angel!'

Much laughter.

There was always one.

Frank decided to ignore it and moved sideways so they could all see the board, he pointed at the more recent incident pictures and shred of paper bearing the number 7. 'As I said, barring the intervention of Saint Michael, I think both of these numbers are references from the Bible. But each is only a single digit, whereas a bible passage would have several.'

Now they were more confused.

'No, I think the numbers found on both victims refer to The Ten Commandments.'

The class Joker spoke up again. 'Oh no, it must be Moses himself!' There were gales of laughter.

He could see what they were thinking. Clearly, the English Detective was two gambas short of a Paella. Or he had been at the loco weed!

Officer Sintes felt he was on a roll. Now that he had got the 'genius' English Detective on the ropes he decided to go in for the final humiliation.

In a patronising tone he asked 'How can you know this? What do the numbers have to do with the Ten Commandments? How can you possibly make such a connection? Just because they are numbers. They could mean anything!'

At his point he turned in his chair and gave his colleagues a smug look as if to say 'Hah, that will teach this clever dick to try and teach Menorca's finest how to suck eggs.'

He looked to Juan who simply shrugged as if he hadn't a clue either. Truth was he did not want to spoil Frank's clincher. He knew that when they heard it, they would be totally convinced too.

Now it was Frank's turn to look smug. He tried to hide it but failed.

'Well…' He began moving back to the first victim scenario. 'This piece of paper was found in the victim's mouth, yes? As you can see it bears what looks like the number 8 on it.' Here he walked to his jacket hanging on the wall and pulled a small King James Bible from a pocket.

Standing back in front of the class, he opened it at a bookmarked page, like a priest about to deliver a sermon, and read the words out aloud.

'*Thou shalt not steal.*' He looked up at them and waited for the penny to drop. Not a flicker yet. He continued…

'That's the 8th Commandment. Thou shalt not steal'

After a few moments he could see some expressions change. They were beginning to get it. 'It was rumoured that the Mayor had been unfairly raising local taxes to line his own pockets.'

Not quite universal clarity yet. Then Bingo, officer Delgado shouted excitedly 'So someone killed him for stealing!'

Frank saw the penny drop for them all.

'Yes. It's possible. And we think it was the same someone who has cropped up in the CCTV footage taken from the last two Fiestas on the days the murders took place. He pointed to some screen grabs taken from the CCTV footage pinned to the board. They appeared to show the same person – a man with a full beard and sunglasses – wearing a combat jacket, and a red baseball cap.

He tapped one of the pictures and said 'We believe this person is referencing one of the Ten Commandments in each killing.

He moved to the St Joan Fiesta crime collage and said 'Which means… that victim two's number, a 7 found under his saddle, refers to…'

This one was easy. Everyone in Menorca knew about Ortega's reputation as a womaniser, and the many rumours of his trysts with young single, and older married women.

'The Seventh Commandment! *Thou shalt not commit adultery.'* Several people said it at the same time and congratulated each other, like schoolchildren who had just learned they had got an A for a Maths paper.

Frank smiled sarcastically at Officer Sintes, who was now not looking so cocky. Now it was Frank who was on a roll.

'Yes. And the spear that killed him was driven through his heart. The heart of a known Casanova. Apt no?'

Someone said 'Could have been worse!' The class convulsed into laughter followed by spontaneous applause.

They all looked at Frank with a new respect. Crazy but a genius. It was obvious now, and it fitted perfectly. Yes. There was a serial killer on the loose. Some sort of religious fanatic with a sick plan to use Menorca festivals as a holy killing ground.

Frank strode over to the third crime scene on the board. 'And at the Fornells Fiesta. Number 6. Anyone?'

'*Thou shalt not kill*. That's the sixth Commandment. I'm sure.' This time it was Juan who piped up.

He got up from his chair and walked over to join Frank at the head of the room. He pointed at the board. The assembled had been scratching their collective heads over the *Don Denaje* label and the photo of the damaged roundabout and crashed cars.

He reminded them of the back-story of Angelica Starr's drink driving conviction, car crash and following demise of the old gentleman in the taxi.

He concluded. 'So, we think the Fiesta Killer, as we are calling him, decided to take revenge and punish Miss Starr by making her drink drain cleaner.'

'Because her drink driving killed the old man!' Officer Delgado concluded triumphantly.

There was silence as they all took this information in. Sage nods and murmurs of agreement. Yes. The pieces of the puzzle fitted.

'What about this suspicious character seen at each of the Fiestas?' Asked a new voice.

'Ah. The bearded gentleman in the red baseball cap. We have witnesses from each Fiesta that remember seeing him on the days of the killings. So, we're pretty sure he's our man.'

The room fell silent. Juan took up the thread again and said 'So, we know who to look out for. We have every reason to believe he will strike again, at another Fiesta, maybe the next one. And that's where we will catch him.'

He looked at them and smiled encouragingly. 'After all, he has committed three murders so far, but there are Ten Commandments.'

ALL QUIET ON THE FIESTA FRONT

The next few weeks went by without incident.

Not that there weren't plenty of crimes and misdemeanors. Some enterprising criminals stole a cash machine from the outside wall of a Supermercado. There were several house fires. 10 burglaries. 14 car crashes. 3 drunken fistfights. And for a change, a *dog* stuck in a tree.

But there were no more Fiesta murders.

Not at the Es Castell or Migjorn Gran Fiestas. There was a serious incident at the Llucmacanes Fiesta involving an ice cream vendor, some local children with angry parents and a subsequent free-for-all brawl. But despite some minor injuries and a broken nose for the vendor (who will be unlikely to overcharge for his Copa Heladas in future) there were no murders.

There was no sign of the figure in the red cap either. So, everyone pretty much figured that The Fiesta Killer had closed the good book on his vengeful killing spree.

It was a week to the next Fiesta and, given the very hot and humid weather, it felt like a good time to kick back and chill for a while.

Frank needed something to take his mind off his troubles. He was not so much bothered about the Fiesta Murders. It was the situation with Marisol. Should he press her to find out more, offer to help or just leave things alone? Would she even be coming back to Menorca? Should he say how much he was missing her? Would there be much point if she wasn't coming back?

He needed time to think. Or, better still, a distraction.

Then one came in the shape of Charles MacKay *aka* Charlie Mack, or rather in the shape of an invite from him to the Theatre to see the Serbian Opera Company. They were touring the Balearics and were presently performing at Mahon's world-famous Teatro Principal.

'Aye. C'mon lad. Ye'll love it.' Charlie had enthused on the phone. 'I've got the tickets and I'll meet you there at 8.'

It was an offer he couldn't refuse. Not that he was an opera fan, unlike his late wife Linda. *Cats* and *Mamma Mia* was about his limit. But this was going to be a welcome step outside of his comfort zone. Something to get his head out of things and forget his problems for a while.

The hill that led up to the Teatro Principal was steep. Even with his walking stick taking much of the strain, Frank found it hard going. Unfortunately, as parking was at a premium in this part of the town, it was also the only sensible way to visit Mahon's famous theatre.

Like most patrons he parked at the bottom of town and made his way up through the winding warren of streets and alleyways to where the imposing building sat at the apex of the Carrer d'en Deià.

He arrived out of breath. There was quite a queue, even though he had taken the trouble to make sure he arrived early. But then, it wasn't every day that the Serbian National Opera was in town.

From outside, the theatre looked pretty much as anyone would have expected anywhere in the world. A collection of unassuming glass-panelled doors. Some wide stone steps. A dimly lit foyer with the ubiquitous deep plush carpet.

But further inside was something very special indeed.

The magnificently restored building, first built in 1829, is the oldest Opera House in Spain. Its interior is a truly breathtaking work of art following the style of Italian theatres, including a neo-classical façade. The auditorium is designed in the shape of a giant horseshoe to ensure excellent acoustics. Seating almost 1000 people, the stalls are surrounded by a series of arches supporting three levels of boxes rising to the most magnificently decorated rotunda ceiling. A work of art in crimson velour preserved in timeless gold leaf aspic.

It was the perfect setting for this special performance of Madame Butterfly by the Serbian troupe who were staging the Puccini Classic.

Charlie Mack was a keen Teatro Principal patron. He had his own box and was a regular attendee. Tickets for this event were like gold dust. But Charlie, being one of the most respected and influential businessmen and benefactors on the island, was always first in the queue for complimentaries.

Not that he was a big opera enthusiast. He just loved the theatre. Several of his ancestors were famous music hall performers and you could say that there was more than a trace of greasepaint in his blood.

Frank stood at the back of the long queue. He leant on his stick and mopped his brow with a hanky. It looked like he would have a bit of a wait. He wondered what Marisol would have made of it. He didn't know if she was an opera fan. For all he knew she may have preferred the cinema or a football match, or even a rock concert. They had never discussed it. How could he know so little about her, yet miss her so much?

To stop sliding back into the painful train of thought he distracted himself by studying the poster on an A-board near the entrance doors. On it was a dramatic scene from the Opera. Inset was a photograph that made him catch his breath. It was the face of a most striking young woman. A cascade of golden hair framed a face of perfect proportions, high cheekbones, full lips and piercing light blue eyes.

Beneath was the caption. 'With Operatic Diva Irina Perkaz.'

He jumped as a familiar voice rose above the hubbub of the queuing punters and startled him from his reverie. 'Hi there. Frank lad. Over here!'

Charlie was waving for him to come over, past the grumbling queue, to the end doorway reserved for VIP guests.

Frank joined him. He pumped Frank's hand with the usual jaunty vigour, then looking over Frank's shoulder asked 'The lass? Not coming? Not an Opera fan?'

'In Madrid. Family business.'

'Och. Shame.' He turned and led the way through the foyer and up a flight of winding stairs with the deepest pile carpet Frank could ever recall walking on.

An official at the head of the stairs simply waved his hand when Charlie reached into his jacket for the tickets. Hell, everybody knew Charlie and what he did for the Arts and this theatre. He needed no ticket. Had never had to show one.

Then they went through a door to Charlie's private box. It was big enough for a half dozen people. But this night it would be just the two of them. They chatted for a while, until the lights went down.

By the third act both men had tears in their eyes. But being old school and very British, they coughed and sniffled as if they had colds coming. Charlie had already been through half a box of tissues.

The performance was powerfully moving. The diva, who played the lead of Madame Butterfly was mesmerizing. That voice. Cutting deep into your soul. That face. So sad it made you feel her pain.

Both men knew they had witnessed something special. Something magical and transcendent. When the performance was over Charlie cleared his throat, wiped his eyes and asked with a croaking voice. 'Did you enjoy it laddie?'

Frank sniffing back his own tears smiled and said.' I didn't think I would. More of a Lloyd Webber man really. But that was amazing. She was wonderful.'

'Aye. She is that.' Charlie blew his nose and then said 'So. Would you like to meet her?'

Frank was a little confused. 'Er…pardon. Meet who?'

Charlie laughed at Frank's puzzled expression.' The Diva of course. Who else? She's an old friend.' He stood and stretched, then suddenly sprang up the steps leading out of the box with the energy of a much younger man. 'Come on.'

Frank joked to himself that Charlie was like an excited youth going on a first date.

They followed the winding circular hallway around to the rear of the stage. It was empty apart from two men who stood chatting near the Star's dressing room. It sounded like Russian. One had a small double-headed eagle tattooed on the side of his neck. He eyed them suspiciously as they approached. Judging by his size and demeanor, Frank assumed he was some kind of bodyguard.

Charlie knocked gently on a dressing room door and called 'Irina. Are ye decent hen? It's Charles Mackay here.' He turned to Frank, winked, and with a whisper said 'Hope we are welcome lad, these diva types can be a bit temperamental after a performance, y'ken.'

Frank could hear music playing somewhere in the room behind the door. It sounded like Elton john. His favourite musical artist. It struck him as odd that an Operatic performer would be listening to pop music. A few lines from *Tiny Dancer* rang in his head. *"Ballerina. You must have seen her. Dancing in the sand.*"

Much to his relief the diva seemed to be in good spirits. A soft female voice with a heavy Slavic accent called back. 'Come on in my darling. But I am not decent you know, so avert your eyes!'

They walked into the dimly lit room. The track playing was in fact *Original Sin*. She turned the music down as they entered. It was a small room and cramped, filled with boxes, clothes racks, shelves lined with shoes and wigs and various glittering accessories. A full-sized mannequin stood in the corner wearing a feather boa and a tiara, and there, seated at a large mirror lit by small bulbs was the Diva herself. Irina Perkaz.

She was wearing a white dressing gown and had her hair wrapped in a towel. Frank could see that the poster hadn't lied. In fact, it hadn't done her justice. Now, without her stage make-up he thought that she had one of the most captivating faces he had ever seen. Her high cheekbones and ice blue eyes gave her an aloof, almost haughty appearance, but this was in sharp contrast with the disarming smile that frequently played on her lips.

She smiled as they entered and held her hand out to Charlie who kissed it with a theatrical bow.

She looked beyond him at Frank. 'And your friend my darling? Who is this handsome young gentleman?'

Frank stepped forward and took her hand too. He wasn't sure if he should also kiss it. It seemed at once formal and yet a little intimate, so he shook it up and down lightly and introduced himself. 'Frank. Frank Harmer. Pleased to meet you Irina. May I say your performance was fantastic.'

'Oh. You liked it did you Frank Frank Harmer?'

'Yes. I thought you were… electric!'

'Why thank you my darling.' She smiled at him and said 'I don't think I have ever been called that before. I like it.' She mulled the word around her mouth like tasting a fine wine. 'Electric. It means very good, yes?'

'Er…yes. I was quite moved.'

Suddenly her face became a frown 'Only quite?'

Now he was embarrassed. 'Ah, no what I meant was…'

She giggled and he realized she was just teasing him. 'I am sorry Frank Frank. It is just my way of…unwinding as they say.'

He smiled. 'No problem.'

She turned her attention once again to Charlie and they spent the next ten minutes catching up and talking about old times. Frank occupied himself by studying the posters on the dressing room walls. Some of them were clearly quite old and almost all featured acts and performers that he had never heard of, with the exception of The Great Caruso.

Then Charlie said suddenly. 'Well I must go now. Let you get on.'

'Of course.' Added Frank. We've taken up enough of your time. You must be exhausted after that stellar performance.'

They said their goodbyes and exchanged polite kisses. This time on the cheeks in the Menorcan way. As they turned to leave, she made a pouting face and in a child-like voice enquired 'What about the tour Charlie? You promised to show me around your beautiful island. Remember?'

Charlie made a tutting sound and snapped his fingers. 'So I did an all. You're not wrong lassie. Trouble is I have to fly to Monaco tomorrow on urgent business. I'll be gone for a week or more.'

He looked troubled and then brightened. 'Wait a minute here.' He turned to Frank and said. 'Perhaps this handsome young man is free to show you the sights? What do ye say Frank?'

Frank felt awkward, and unsure how to respond. 'Well, I er... the fact is I have…'

'Frank! You wouldna disappoint this beautiful young lassie now would ye? It would be a crying shame as she has come all this way to sing for us so sweetly.' Charlie Mack batted his eyes at Frank in fun.

Frank laughed and nodded. Why not? He was at a loose end. He needed a distraction. And anyway, this could be fun.

He smiled charmingly at the Diva.

'It will be my pleasure.'

FIESTA DES SANT LORENC. 'HALF DEAD'

The pretty town of Alaior is situated just off the main road that runs the length of the island.

Most of this old town has been built on a hill with the main streets leading up to the beautiful 14th Century Santa Eulàlia church at its top. It is a busy working town with the thriving Zona Industrial Alaior business park. Here you will find warehouses, offices and factories for everything from cheese production to truck sales. Also, furniture stores, supermarkets and cafés.

On any given weekday Alaior is a hive of activity. A proper working town. But not so much during the second weekend of August each year when many factories and shops shut down for the annual Fiesta of Sant Lorenc.

During this long weekend Menorcan equestrian displays and races take place amongst its weaving labyrinth of streets, along with the usual marching bands, with dancing, drinking and singing.

It all culminates in the Parade of Floats. Each year they choose a different theme. Sometimes it features floats bearing tableaus from the towns historic and military past, complete with authentic looking costumes and props. Sometimes the theme is from popular Menorcan sports or pastimes.

This year the theme is *Menorca. Under the Waves*, celebrating the fact that since 1993 Menorca has been a designated UNESCO Biosphere Reserve, and its clear surrounding Mediterranean waters are a haven for marine life, teeming with a huge variety of species.

On this warm Sunday evening, Frank Harmer is among the excited crowd lining the street along the Carrer des Ramal, the town's main high street. He would have invited opera diva Irina Perkaz to join him as this would have been a great way to kick off their 'island tour'. But that will have to wait as it is business as usual in Mahon and she has a performance this evening.

He is sitting on one of the stone benches in the Plaça des Ramal. This delightful pedestrianised square, edged at the roadside by stone planters filled with seasonal flowers, is ideally placed to rest and catch one's breath on your way up to the church or post office. It is home to small pastry shops, cafés and a corner newsagent, and is an oasis of coolness and calm on a hot day, with welcome shade provided by a central group of Orange trees.

Everyone is waiting for the parade to start. It has been a very warm day and the evening air is still and heavy. Luckily, Frank is dressed very lightly for the occasion, so he isn't feeling too oppressed by the closeness of his fellow men and women gathered here. There are several other people squashed onto the bench with him. The old woman next to him smells of Lavender and bleach. She is chatting away to her husband sat next to her. He is nodding but not really listening and puffing away on his pipe.

Nearby, people are crowded onto the ridiculously narrow pavement of this street, trying to position themselves for the best view as they wait for the parade. They jostle and chatter excitedly as they hear distant strands of sounds that indicate it will be approaching soon around the end of this sloping street.

Plain clothes policemen are amongst the crowd and dotted all along the parade route. All are discreetly armed and briefed to look out for the tell-tale red cap of the Fiesta Killer.

Officer Juan should have been here too but is now making his way on foot from a local garage having had a burst tyre. He is keeping in touch with his men and Frank by phone.

The instruction is to keep a low profile. To try and spot the killer and catch him in the act. At least, that is the plan. But, as with the last few Fiestas, he may not show today.

They also have little more than the red cap, beard and combat jacket to go on. What if he changes his clothes this time? Or has decided to shave off his beard?

More to the point, where and when is he likely to strike? Who will be his intended victim?

There is no way of knowing. They will just have to wait and see.

Frank has a feeling in his gut that the Fiesta Killer will be making an appearance today, and Juan has said that if he does then they are sure to nab him in the act. Frank is not so certain but hopes it will be the case.

Just after 8.40 there is a sudden increase in noise and activity as the parade rolls into view at the bottom of the street. The music is a mishmash of pop songs from the floats and the jaunty sea shanty coming from the Tannoy speakers, hung on both sides of the street.

People jostle and crane their necks to get a view. Children run about excitedly. People clap and shout. His bench companions stand on it so they can see over the heads of the crowd. Frank will need to join them if he wants to watch the Parade clearly, but his leg isn't quite up to the task after the long walk here. So, with the aid of his walking stick, he stands slowly and goes to find a gap in the crowd at the kerb.

Luckily, one of the plain clothed officers is standing on the steps in the doorway of the newsagents and waves him over to join her.

From the steps they have a good view of the floats as they go by. They are really good. First is *On the Sea Bed* with a sunken ship and treasure chest wrapped in the tentacles of a giant Octopus. There is also a large 'bed' with children in it dressed as crabs, clams and prawns. A lot of curtain material has gone into that thinks Frank.

Next comes *In the court of King Neptune*. A large bare - chested man, with a cape, crown and trident is sat on a giant half-shell throne, attended by scantily clad mermaids.

Frank is impressed and he claps.

Several more floats go by with various marine and nautical scenes. They all have banners bearing the theme title and a credit for the organisation or sponsor. *The Marie Celeste* features the pupils and teachers of Alaior Primary School. *Pirates of the Caribbean* comes from the staff of the Coinga Cheese factory. *The Little Mermaid* by a local Peluquería (hairdressing) salon.

All receive the rapturous applause and delight of the crowd, many recognising and calling out to children and friends aboard the mobile scenarios. Then comes a float with a scene that draws gasps from the crowd.

It is the creation of the Son Bou diving centre *Buceo de Marco* (Marco's Scuba Centre). It is entitled *Jaws* and is very impressive. A great white shark, so realistic that it could have been borrowed from the set of the classic Spielberg film, is chewing through the back end of a boat. The occupant of which is disappearing head-first into its open mouth.

Only the wetsuit clad diver's bottom half can be seen - legs and flippered feet sticking out from between the large white incisors.

This is accompanied by the ominous pulsing movie soundtrack. Dah-duh! Dah-duh! Which steadily increases in tempo. The crowd love it. They laugh and cheer wildly.

This is the best one so far. So realistic. The man in the shark's mouth does not move or even twitch. This is clearly Marco - the sole proprietor and staff member of the Scuba Centre.

Everyone in Alaior knows Marco. He is a very experienced diver and a popular local character. He is a larger than life personality with a loud infectious laugh. He is given to self-promotion and often seen in the local papers carrying out some crazy publicity stunt or making wild claims on local radio, saying he has found sunken treasure or spotted a giant squid. All to attract publicity for his business.

His promotions aim to get people to book his Scuba excursions, with offers like his popular Scuba Sunday Specials. Offering discounted family dives.

Some church leaders frown on this. But they understand that a little dispensation is in order within this holiday economy. They know with seasonal businesses you have to make hay while the sun shines. Or in this case Scuba Excursions on summer Sundays.

Also, Marco is such a colourful character, it is hard not to like him.

He turns up at all the local fetes, summer fairs and Christmas concerts. He raises money for local charities. 'Marco? Oh yes. What a good guy. A little crazy but always game for a laugh.'

So, there is little doubt that the legs protruding from the gaping jaws of the monster belong to Marco, and there is much laughter because of this. 'Oh look. There is Marco. Who else would stick his head in the mouth of a shark?'

Then the float stops suddenly. A child has run out into the street right in front of the parade's lead vehicle.

The momentum makes the *Jaws* float lurch forward and 'Marco' is ejected from the giant fish's mouth and onto the bed of the truck. But to the horror of the crowd it is only the bottom half of the man.

There are mixed reactions from the onlookers. Some think this is another excellent stunt *a la Marco* and applaud the very realistic looking dummy he has used.

Others are not so sure as it is *too* realistic, especially as there is what looks like a slick of blood and some innards now stretching from the marine beast's cavernous mouth.

Their worst fears are confirmed as the truck jerks forward once more and the detached lower torso slides down over the side of the float and onto the ground - spattering the shoes and shins of those stood nearest with blood and gore.

The float moves on. Its driver is blissfully unaware of the horror show that has transpired behind him on his vehicle.

Cheers now turn to screams. Their cries and shouts are counter-pointed by the lively cacophony of sound from the next float as it arrives, blaring out the soundtrack from Disney's Bedknobs and Broomsticks - *'Bobbing Along at the Bottom of the Briny Sea.'*

Shocked parents cover their children's eyes and herd them hurriedly away.

Further back along the route people are unaware of what has transpired and continue to cheer the parade along.

But around the severed half of the diver now lying by the kerb at the Plaça des Ramal there is total panic and confusion.

Old Amalio, stood on the stone bench thinks this is all part of the show. He laughs and elbows his wife to get her attention.

'Did you see that? Good old Marco. This is better than the cinema. How does he do it?'

His wife cannot speak. She is trying not to vomit as she turns to face him. Much to her husband's regret, she does not succeed.

To Frank it was like watching a movie scene unfold in slow motion.

People were screaming and running in every direction. Children were crying, not really understanding what was going on.

He felt rooted to the spot and unable to move, or even process what was unfolding before his eyes. Yes, he had expected something to happen. But this had caught him totally off-guard.

His step buddy too.

She grabbed his arm and uttered a loud oath. It shook him out of his torpor. 'Come on, we've got to clear this area and secure the crime scene.'

She got on her phone and informed the rest of the team. The both of them went to where the body, or the half of it that had dropped off the float, lay. The float itself had come to rest once more a little further up the street. The driver was now leaning out of his cab and staring back in disbelief.

Some people, those with strong stomachs, were gathering around the semi-torso on the ground, contents and blood pooling around its waist.

To his horror Frank saw that someone was about to reach down and check that it was a real person. He could not let that happen as it would taint potential forensic evidence and he shouted at the man as he ran toward the scene. 'Stop! Police! Don't touch that body.'

The startled group parted as he approached.

The horrific news was now spreading along the street like wildfire. Fearing that in the ensuing panic someone might get injured, his police colleague began trying to calm the situation down. She displayed her badge and with calm and firm authority told people to move away down the street.

Frank looked around for something to cover the half body and saw that the large banner on the nearest float would be ideal. As he climbed aboard to retrieve it, someone watching from a shop doorway across the street caught his eye. A man with a beard, wearing a combat jacket and red baseball cap! He looked just like the one in the CCTV footage.

Frank felt his heart skip a beat. He couldn't help but stare. The figure noticed this and for a moment their eyes met.

It was strange, but there seemed to be a startled look of recognition from the man. He pulled down the peak of his cap, hauled up his jacket collar, then left the doorway and began walking quickly away up the hill.

Frank was unsure what to do but knew he could not let the fellow get away.

With adrenaline pumping, he jumped down from the float and gave chase. He did not want to lose sight of the fleeing figure who was now beginning to run, pushing people in his way off the narrow kerb. Frank increased his pace and began shouting for people to get out of the way. He reached for his phone and called Juan.

There was no time for pleasantries. 'Juan it's Frank. I've spotted Red Cap. He's making a break for it up the hill. On Carrer des Ramal, coming up from the Plaça.'

By chance, Juan was already making his way down from the top of the street. He was already aware of the horror that had taken place further down and had instructed his men to clear the area and wait for him to get there.

He had taken a short cut from the Zona Industrial which came out near the top of the Carrer des Ramal and saved a long walk around.

He stopped next to the stationary line of floats that stood like a sleeping and garishly coloured anaconda snaking down the hill. He peered into the melee further down. People were still running around, some in costumes from their tableaus, some spectators holding their young and hurrying away, people on their phones spreading the news, some even videoing the grisly crime scene.

There! Just past the Tobacconist's. Someone in a red cap heading his way. He was approaching at a fast pace, still pushing past the people on the kerb.

Juan stepped into a doorway to hide and wait, intending to step out and challenge the suspect when he got near. He drew his weapon. The man was possibly armed. He certainly would be if it was the Fiesta Killer. If it wasn't him, why was he running away?

Before he ducked into the recess, he spotted Frank following behind the man in the distance. Good. Between them they would have him trapped. But the man seemed to have a sixth sense. Just as he was no more than 10 feet away, he stopped suddenly, turned back and caught sight of Frank hurrying after him.

This gave Juan the opportunity he needed. He stepped out from the doorway and shouted at the figure. 'Stop! Armed police! Put your hands in the air and turn around slowly!'

For a second Red Cap froze, then he suddenly sprang into action, dashing through the space between two parked floats and across to the other side of the street.

Juan chased after him through the gap and onto the kerb at the other side. The man was running up the hill once more and had quite a lead on him. Then he stopped and disappeared into a narrow side street.

This heartened the pursuing policeman who knew that the street was a dead end. There was no way through. Just a solid high brick wall at the far end. Red Cap wasn't going anywhere!

They had cornered the Fiesta killer!

Juan stopped at the mouth of the street and waited for Frank to join him. He arrived out of breath and looked very flushed. His leg hadn't troubled him too much on the way up, adrenaline had seen to that, but he knew he would pay a price later on.

'He went down here.' He jerked a thumb at the alleyway. 'But he can't get away. It's a dead end.' Juan pointed up at the street sign which showed a graphic of this fact.

'Right.' He waved at Frank to stay put and said. 'You wait here while I go and see if I can talk him into surrendering.'

Frank thought this might not be the best plan and said 'Don't you think you should wait for back up? He may well be armed.'

Juan smiled reassuringly and showing the police revolver said 'Don't worry my friend, I know how to use this. And I won't hesitate if I have to.' This last part he said loudly for the benefit of the desperado hiding in the alley. Secretly Juan hated guns and hoped he would never have to use one, again.

Without waiting for further protestation from the Englishman he walked slowly but steadily into the dead-end street. Staying close to the walls.

It was narrow, and the tall terraced houses made it quite dark. The street looked empty. There was no sign of the fleeing suspect. None of the doorways were recessed so he could see that there was nowhere for the man to hide. Odd?

It was also a short street, no more than 70 meters long, with a solid 10 ft high brick wall at the end, topped with broken glass. Against the end wall stood the usual row of large *Basura* waste and recycling bins.

Juan crept slowly along watching and listening for any movement or sound. Suddenly a door opposite him opened. He dropped to one knee, pointing the weapon.

The small woman holding the cat shrieked and ran back inside, slamming the door behind her. Juan stood up slowly, cursing under his breath and tried to gulp his heart back down into his chest.

He looked back down the street just in time to catch sight of the man in the red cap climbing up onto the large green Basura bin. Clearly, he had been hiding behind it and was now attempting to get over the tall wall and make his escape.

Juan holstered the gun and began to run. If he was quick enough, he could grab the man and pull him to the ground. Dios, the man was quick! He was also very limber judging by the way he was scaling the wall. A match for Spiderman!

By the time Juan had got there, the man was halfway over the top of the wall. Climbing onto the bin, he just managed to grab the fellow's left leg before he could hoist himself completely over. He got a pretty good grip, but only to receive the guy's right foot in his face for his trouble. This sent him falling backwards off the bin and crashing to the ground, still clutching the absconding killer's trainer in his hand.

He lay there catching his breath and staring angrily up at the top of the wall. The bad guy was gone. He hoped his men were waiting on the other side but doubted they had got there in time. It was then he noticed something small and green hanging from the broken glass on the wall top. It looked like a piece of torn cloth.

He walked slowly from the alleyway. Frank, who had been keeping in touch with the team, told him there was no sign of the suspect anywhere. He had got clean away.

'Well not quite clean.' Juan showed him his recent battle spoils. One well-worn Nike trainer and a ragged piece of the guy's Tee shirt, presumably torn off as the man hoisted himself over the wall.

They noticed there was some blood on it. 'He must have cut himself on the broken glass.' Offered Juan. Adding with a sour note 'That'll teach the wily bastard.'

Juan sat down heavily on the kerb edge. He looked crestfallen, so Frank said 'Well, it's something to go on. Perhaps forensics will get a DNA match.'

They wouldn't.

But they did find another clue inside the Shark's mouth.

Along with the upper half of the unfortunate wetsuit clad Marco, inside the pipe of the snorkel he was wearing, they found a rolled-up piece of paper with another number on it.

The number 4.

'WHAT HAPPENS IN BINISAFUA'

They started Irina's tour of the island with a trip to the top of Monte Toro, Menorca's only mountain, standing at over 1100 ft high at the centre of the island. Frank thought it would be a good place to begin as, with a Panoramic view, you could see the whole of Menorca.

As they stood in a viewing area near the summit, he pointed out many of the landmarks and towns. The bays and the lighthouses. It was a breathtaking view and she was most impressed.

They took a cruise around the island in a glass-bottomed boat. Irina said she felt a little seasick in the confined observation area below deck. But she seemed to enjoy the sight of the many shoals of colourful fish. They even saw a pod of Dolphins and she squealed with delight as they swam past the windows.

He took her shopping to the designer outlets and stores at Ferreries and Mercadal. She bought a hat and some Avarcas (Menorcan Sandals) and a pink candy-striped shirt that she thought would look good on him (Frank thought it a bit garish but said he loved it).

They visited historic buildings and ancient Talaiot monuments.

They dined at some of Menorca's finest restaurants (Charlie had insisted that they put everything on his tab).

They danced the night away at the Xoroi Caves clifftop nightspot.

They laughed. They sang. They drank. She seemed able to drink copious amounts of her favourite tipple – Vodka and Cranberry Juice. Frank tried to match her in Scotches but regretted it the next morning.

Over the weeks they became good friends.

This was in spite of the ubiquitous presence of her gofer, the ever-present Goran.

He was the same a surly looking character that he had seen by Irina's dressing room. The one with a double-headed eagle tattoo on his neck. Mean and muscular looking, it was easy to see why Irina had employed him as both baggage hauler and her personal bodyguard.

His cold dark eyes took everything in slowly as if it were a threat. They surveyed Frank with distain. Not that he ever said anything offensive or insulting to Frank, but he could tell the man disliked him intensely.

If he didn't know any better, he would have said that Goran was more than a little jealous of his friendship with Irina. But then, the personal dislike was mutual. Especially as he had the infuriating habit of accompanying Irina everywhere they went.

He spoke very little English. At least he gave everyone that impression. He seemed to communicate mainly in grunts. So, conversation between them was kept at an absolute minimum. Which was more than agreeable with Frank.

He realised one day that they had not done the one essential thing that is part of the Menorca experience. A picnic on the beach (ideally without Goran in tow). Followed by a swim and snorkel. She loved the idea.

Frank, a keen snorkeler himself, said there could only be one place that would fit the bill. Binisafua Cala.

This narrow inlet is just a half-mile long, and being edged by steep rocky outcrops topped by clusters of hanging pine trees, it is very pretty.

Popular with the locals, family groups can be found on its small sandy beach on sunny days, mostly in the late afternoon and cooler evening hours.

The water gets deep quite quickly when you swim out from the shore, but being a very sheltered Cala, it is almost always calm and clear. So, it affords perfect conditions for snorkeling, fishing and the mooring of yachts and boats. Although, this bijou bay can easily become a little crowded with crafts in high season if too many sailing excursions get the same idea on the same day.

Today, being late August and nearing the end of the peak tourist season, it was not such a day. Just the odd Menorcan Llaut moored here and there. But it was warm and sunny and ideal for picnicking and bathing.

Fortunately, Goran had begged off the trip owning to an

injured hand he got playing a drinking game with some of the others in the Serbian troupe.

They left the car in the narrow parking strip just off the main road and walked to the path entrance that led steeply down through trees to the beach. The way was uneven with rough hand-made steps, edged with olivewood branches.

Irina, dressed in a cotton floral summer dress and wide brimmed sun hat, led the way. Frank, carrying the fully laden picnic basket, beach umbrella and beach blanket, struggled manfully in her wake.

The diva was in good spirits and chatted constantly. Not that Frank was listening. He was thinking about Marisol. To be honest, he felt a little guilty about spending so much time with Irina while Marisol was away dealing with a stressful family situation. Should he really be enjoying himself so much?

They found a nice flat spot in the shade at the corner of the beach. Frank removed a few large stones and pebbles and put down the picnic blanket. Irina unpacked her snorkel from her small pink backpack then began undressing.

Frank, being a gentleman turned away and, feeling awkward, looked around expansively and said 'Ahh. The perfect place for some R and R.'

He then busied himself with the hamper, opened it and took out his own swim shorts and snorkel which had been neatly wrapped in a towel and tucked in the lid pocket. 'Well, what do you think? Paradise or wha...'

As he raised his head and looked up, words just fell away and his breath left his body. She stood there before him in one of the skimpiest polkadot bikinis he had ever seen. She was tall and quite statuesque in build, which emphasized the smallness of the bikini even more. The phrase *itsy bitsy teeny weeny* ran through his brain.

He stood there open mouthed.

She laughed at his stunned expression. He looked like a goldfish that someone had just tipped out of a jar.

She twirled 360 and asked impishly 'Well, what do you think darling? Will I do?'

Frank's brain tried to process this question, but it was not possible with all the other competing information flooding in from his optical cortex.

He thought she looked like Aphrodite rising from the waves on the half-shell. Perfect in proportion from her cascading blonde hair to her curvy hips sporting a tattoo of a small red flower. A Peony Frank thought.

There was one just one small blemish on this most perfect of bodies. A long pink and old looking scar just below her belly button. Frank noticed it as his gaze travelled downward. He jumped when she said. 'Naughty boy. Don't you know it is rude to stare!'

Deeply embarrassed he looked away, mumbled an apology and began busying himself with the important business of erecting the beach umbrella. She just giggled and kicked some sand at him.

Suddenly he felt stupid. Why was he so embarrassed? Why were the English so reserved and prudish? He wasn't in Clacton-on-Sea now. He was on a secluded beach on a Balearic island. Heck, some of the locals didn't even bother with swimwear here.

He was a native of Menorca now, so surely the old adage applied here. *When in Menorca do as the Menorcans do.*

No dammit, time to let all that stuffy British reserve nonsense go. Time for some uninhibited fun in the sun. He picked up his towel and flicked it at her bottom.

She laughed and picked up his swim shorts, ran to the water's edge, and waving them at him shouted 'You will have to catch me if you want to get them back!'

'Why you little....' He grinned and then quickly slipped off his own clothes and ran after her. To hell with the English.

They ran into the clear cool water together, splashing each other and laughing like children.

They swam out along the Cala. The water got colder but not unpleasantly so. About halfway along, and around 5 meters deep, they stopped to snorkel.

Shoals of Sea Bream and small exotically coloured little fish swam beneath them among the many outcrops of rock that littered the Cala floor. Swathes of seagrass danced languidly in the ebb and flow of the slow currents. Every now and then a flatfish – a dab or ray - would wriggle out from the sand or back into it to be camouflaged, as they dove down for a closer look at the sea bed and its occupants.

Irina spotted a large Starfish and waved to Frank to come and see. He was just about to surface and get another lungful of air, so he gave her a thumbs up sign and did so. Surfacing above her he got the air and dived back down. On his decent he could see her body beneath him, dappled with sunlight and her golden hair caressing the water.

He thought she looked like a mermaid.

He felt a pang of guilt once more and pushed the thought away as he joined her for a close-up examination of the Starfish. She had a look of delight on her face. She was really enjoying this. He smiled and gave her another thumbs up sign. She pointed upwards and they both swam to the surface.

Treading water and sucking in the fresh air she said breathlessly. 'This is all so marvelous. Thank you for bringing me here Frank. You are such a lovely man.' And with that she moved closer and put her arms around his neck.

They looked into each other's eyes. All other thoughts - Marisol and Fiesta Murders - evaporated from his mind. Now there was only Irina, the water, the sunlight and the warm sea breeze.

He went to say something. To pay her some compliment.

She simply smiled and said 'Shut up and kiss me darling.'

Well, he reasoned, what kind of fool could resist this beautiful and free-spirited woman. It would be positively rude to refuse. Wouldn't it? Besides, 'what happens in Binisafua stays in Binisafua'. Shouldn't that be the rule here?

Their lips met and he felt her body, warm and soft against his own. Treading water, the embrace and the kiss became more passionate. Pulling back, he gazed into her eyes and said with a husky voice 'Irina. Do you think maybe we, I mean do you think you and I should...'

He did not finish the question as suddenly she jerked rigid and, with a terrified look in her eyes, let out a loud scream.

It was not the reaction he was expecting.

She swam away from him, turning, arms flailing. Then he saw the source of her anguish. Bobbing along, just breaking the surface of the water near where she had just been was the telltale dome of a large Medusa. It had clearly stung her back and shoulders and maybe lower down, judging by the way she was trying to reach behind her in the water.

He swam around the creature and, carefully taking her arm, helped her back to the shore with her cursing in Serbian and English all the way. 'Sranje! Kopile! The bastard stung me!'

He sat her down on the blanket and quickly got an icepack from the hamper and held it against the stings. They were nasty looking. Like angry lines of burnt flesh running across her back diagonally from waist to shoulder. He wrapped the icepack in a towel and dabbed her wounds gently as she sat on the sand hugging her knees and sobbing, cursing frequently.

All thoughts of romance now evaporated. Paradise was definitely lost for today.

Or at least it was going to have to be postponed.

LA FIESTA DE SANT LLUIS. 'DEAD BOLT'

It is the Sunday afternoon of the Sant Lluis Fiesta weekend. It has been warm and sunny. But now thunder is in the air and black clouds are building above the parade, which is in full swing along the town's main avenue.

Being late August, the weather is usually fine. But with the island's high humidity, thunderstorms are not uncommon at this time of year. They are short lived affairs. But they can come on very suddenly and be very violent, and the rainfall very heavy. Heavy enough to put a premature end to today's festivities.

At the edge of Sant Lluis stands a Moli. An old Menorcan windmill. So old, it is no longer in operation but has been lovingly preserved, like many on the island, as a testament to a bygone age. It looks incongruous sat amongst the modern squared-up streets and box like buildings. They look drab in comparison to its bright blue shutters, white walls and jaunty wooden sails - looking like jolly sailor's arms waving to an approaching ship.

It's a great tourist attraction that looks good on travel brochures and postcards. It has been closed for repairs for several weeks, but today it hasn't stopped someone from sneaking in and climbing its rickety wooden spiral staircase to get a good view over the Fiesta.

This figure is standing at the glassless window opening, partially hidden by the blue shutters, holding a crossbow which is loaded and ready for firing. The bowman surveys the crowds below with an expert eye, searching for a particular target. One that the killer has marked out for death.

Ah, there he is! The Policeman. The chain-smoker. The one that has been getting too close and has to go. But it must look good. All part of the 'Fiesta Killer's' vengeful biblical vendetta.

The officer is stood at the street corner opposite, on the junction over which the shadow of the Moli stretches. He is conveniently illuminated by a streetlamp that has come on in the prematurely failing light, making the job of targeting him so much easier.

Unlike the rifle, this crossbow is only equipped with a standard daylight scope. The assassin wasn't expecting it to be quite so dark. The thunderclouds have turned day to dusk.

The Officer is talking to someone on his phone. He is lighting yet another cigarette. That would be the death of him, thinks the bowman, if he wasn't about to get a bolt from the blue!

As if to accentuate his punchline a sudden stab of lightening splits the air and thunder booms. Rain begins to fall in large marble sized drops. Better hurry before the victim leaves! The killer raises the weapon. Finger on trigger, and finds the victim in the crosshairs of the site.

The bolt is a 16inch steel arrow and is sharply barbed. Wrapped around it is a note. Another Biblical reference from the 'crazed' serial killer! The number 9. The ninth commandment.

The bowman chuckles quietly. That should make them think! It should throw them off the scent before the big one. The one that this person has been planning for so long.

There is no way the expert marksman can miss. A kill is guaranteed. But before the bowman can let loose the deadly shaft, another arc of electricity splits the air. The light from a billion volts bounces off every metal and glass surface in the street and dazzles the shooters eyes.

The flash illuminates the Moli window and the silhouette of its occupant catches the keen eye of the detective. He just happens to be looking toward the windmill as he is instructing his men to stand down. The rainstorm is sure to bring an abrupt end to proceedings.

The finger tightens on the trigger. With a sharp twang the bolt leaves the bow and flies at bullet speed toward its target.

With an instinct bred by many years in the field, the policeman throws himself backward, twisting to the left, just as the barbed tip of the bolt tears through his jacket at the shoulder, ripping cloth and flesh and chipping bone.

He hits the ground heavily and lies still. The bolt embeds its point in the front door of the house behind him. Juan yells from his prone position for everyone to get down, then rolls backwards, deeper into the doorway. He quickly stands, flattening himself against the door, out of the line of fire of the madman in the Moli.

The bolt's shaft is sticking out of the door.
He sees the blood on it and then realises he has been hit.
His blood creating a rosette on his jacket at the shoulder.
He also sees there is something wrapped around the shaft, tied with some twine.

Another Biblical note no doubt. Forgetting crime scene protocol, he reaches over and retrieves it. At the same time his men, hearing his shouts have cleared the area and are in position, weapons drawn, at the base of the Moli.

He signals for them to approach with caution, pointing up at the blue shutters. But he knows that by now the would-be assassin will have vacated the premises.

He relaxes a little, reaches for a cigarette with trembling hand, lights it and then unravels and examines the paper note.

A crudely drawn number 9 is on the inside. Nine? What was the ninth commandment again? Adultery? No. He would have remembered doing that one. Ah yes. 'Thou shalt not bear false witness…'

False witness? Against who? It doesn't make any sense. Perhaps the shooter has made a mistake. But then, he isn't playing with a full deck.

Now the pain starts as the blood loss increases and the adrenaline wears off. His head begins to swim and he sits down awkwardly in the doorway.

Coming over and seeing his injury, one of his men calls for

an ambulance. Juan does not feel that this is justified. It is not so bad, just flesh wound.

He looks at the note again. He will work out the meaning later, but he has no doubt. He was the intended target. That bolt was meant to kill him or frighten him off.

Well he has picked on the wrong cop.

Now Juan is angry. Now he is more determined than ever to catch the Fiesta Killer and bring him to justice.

Now it is personal.

LAZY SUNDAY

They sat sipping cold beers outside the little beach bar at Binibeca. Its tables cleverly arranged on flat areas of the rocky promontory that sloped down to the sea at the corner of the bay.

The late morning sun played teasingly with the small waves that ambled in. A gentle breeze took the edge off the rising heat. Sea birds swooped and squawked at the children playing and adults paddling at the water's edge. It was a perfect day.

They sat in silence for a while, just enjoying the moment. Both lost in thought. After a while Irina spoke. Not turning her gaze from the horizon she asked 'Do you have someone Frank?'

Frank was thinking about another time he was here. The case of the body washed up in the red tide of jellyfish.

The question took him completely by surprise. 'Er…how do you mean, someone?'

'Someone special in your life. A girlfriend…. a lover here in Menorca.'

He gave her a questioning look and she added 'You are a single man. A handsome and eligible widower. I should have thought…'

Now he was embarrassed. 'Well…I…not really. I mean…I have some close friends…' He thought about mentioning Marisol but there didn't seem much point. Besides, he was growing quite fond of Irina and wondered if there could be something starting with her.

He shook his head and asked 'You? Is there anyone?'

'She shook her head and smiled 'No. Not at the moment.'

'And has there ever been a Mr Perkaz? Children?'

Suddenly, it was as if a dark shadow had passed over her. There was a distant look in her eyes. She sighed and folded her arms, hugging herself. There was sadness in her voice as she said 'That is a long story. And not a happy one.'

He decided not to enquire further. The day was going so well, it seemed a shame to spoil the mood. Instead he made a mock serious face and said 'Well. What a pair of sad souls we are.'

She brightened at this. 'Huh? We are like two fish?'

He realized she thought he meant 'Soles' but let it go and thought that it was a good time to find out if he was in with a chance. He reached across the table and let his hand rest lightly on her arm. She did not pull away but just sat there smiling warmly at him.

He felt a little nervous, but knew that, sitting here in this little corner of heaven, it was the ideal moment. He looked into her eyes, plucked up courage and said 'Perhaps it is time we took this relationship to another level?'

Her reaction was not at all what he expected. After a few seconds of blank expression, as if she was trying to process this information, she suddenly burst into hysterical laughter. It was as if she had just got the punchline of the funniest joke in the world.

People at other tables looked over.

When she had finally stopped laughing, she clapped her hands together and said 'Oh darling. That is priceless!'

Frank flushed with embarrassment. He looked around and smiled sheepishly at the onlookers as if they had been sharing a funny story.

She saw his discomfort and said 'I am sorry. I do not mean to be unkind. I am very flattered, of course. But you must know that this cannot be anything more than…' She searched for the right word 'A fling. Fun. Nothing more.'

Realising his mistake he tried to make light of it and mumbled a few inanities. But she could see he was disappointed. 'Sorry darling. But it could never work. We come from two different worlds. I like you very much, of course. But I could never settle down. My career means too much to me. It needs all my attention and commitment. There is no room for… anything serious.'

She gave him a sympathetic smile, held his hand and said 'Let us just enjoy our time together as good friends.'

He was nodding absently as she said this. But inside he felt foolish. How could he have misread the signs? Idiot!

Not wishing to cause him further anguish, she decided to change the subject. 'So. This case you are working on. Are there any leads yet? Have you a suspect?'

Frank was thankful for this change of tack and, even though he was not supposed to talk about the case, he could not see the harm in telling Irina a few details.

Besides, he reasoned, much of it was public knowledge by now anyway. It had been reported extensively in the local media.

He told her all about the progress they were making and what they knew about The Fiesta Killer - his MO of biblical vengeance and cryptic paper clues. The red baseball cap, combat jacket and beard. The near fatal attempt on inspector Juan.

She seemed fascinated and gasped or shook her head, asking questions as the tale unfolded.

Frank felt this was just her way of helping to expunge the crime of the previous romantic discourse, but he was grateful for the distraction and was soon feeling much better.

He went on at length about the case, how they planned to catch the killer at the next Fiesta – the big one at Mahon. Then he told her of some of his other exploits regarding Menorcan crime cases where he had assisted the local Police, until the familiar figure of Goran hove into view, waving and shouting from the top road car park where he had dropped them earlier.

Frank's heart sank at his arrival. As it always did. But this time it also gave him the idea for a joke. He said 'Perhaps it's for the best anyway. Well, we would only have had to adopt little Goran.'

She thought that was hysterical too, and they laughed all the way up the beach path to the car park.

'THE MOZAMBIQUE DRILL'

Inspector Juan Rodriguez sat on a rock and watched the small waves make slow progress up the pretty sandy beach of Cala Mitjana. It was one of his favourite thinking spots, and he often came here when a case got tough and he needed to do some uninterrupted mental reviewing.

Despite the lovely sunny day, the beach was quite empty, aside from a few walkers and gulls fighting over the remains of a dead fish washed up at the water's edge.

The wound on his shoulder had put him on sick leave for a week, so he had time for some R and R. He decided to go over everything he knew about the Fiesta Killer case, starting with the first murder.

It was baffling. After visiting that particular crime scene and interviewing those who had been present at the incident, the investigating team had got no further in finding the person responsible.

He lit a cigarette, took a deep drag and set his mind to

analysing the problem. Okay. What *did* they have? *Motive*: There may have been some disgruntled taxpayers who would have wanted to make an example of the Mayor. But by killing him?

It was also feasible that someone may have been pissed-off enough to have kidnapped the Mayor and dressed him up as a rag doll to 'teach him a lesson' and to give him a scare.

There were some interviewed who expressed their anger and dissatisfaction with Mayor Alfonso. But all of them had denied having any part in an actual 'prank' that quite literally had misfired. Yet *someone* had killed him. Someone had shot him dead and left a little message for them to find. But who?

Had anyone seen someone suspicious? Not really. One or two had mentioned seeing an unfamiliar face. Some said a short man, some said tall, some said clean shaven and some said with a beard. But that was about it. The usual poor recall embellished by imagination that followed such incidents.

Right. *Means*: The Council Chambers had been shut, as usual, for the duration of the Easter holidays. So, there must have been plenty of opportunities for anyone to have kidnapped and doped the Mayor, trussed him up as a rag doll and then hung him on the frame for the traditional 'shoot the guy'.

Apparently, according to his wife, the Mayor had planned to go fishing for the weekend with some of his chums. 'Fishing' being a euphemism for going on the booze and playing cards. Although, neither his wife nor anyone else had heard from him over the period. She just assumed he had gone to their holiday Finca - the holiday cottage they own at the quiet northern inlet of Cala Morell - and he had simply switched his phone off.

However, none of his usual cohorts said they had been with him that weekend. He hadn't turned up as arranged and they had simply assumed he had changed his mind or was ill. So that left a 24 to 36hour gap when anyone could have taken him, drugged him and under the cover of darkness placed him in the deserted spot where the *shoot the guy* ceremony always took place.

That left the *Method*: 'Shot in the head and chest'. Again, it could have been any of the shooters. Of course, they all denied using live rounds. All claimed to have been firing blanks. There was no match found between any weapon capable of firing live rounds and the bullets that killed him. So, where did the live rounds come from? Who fired the three fatal shots, one to the head and two to the… wait a minute!

He stood up suddenly as the realisation hit him. He dropped the cigarette into the sand, and phoned the officer in charge of the investigating team.

Yes. The officer confirmed that there had indeed been one shot to the head and two to the chest.

If he was right, they all might have missed the real evidence here. The clue that could help them track down the identity of the Fiesta Killer.

The Mozambique Drill! Could it be so?
He decided to call Frank and run his theory by him.

If anyone could confirm his suspicions it was Frank.

Frank hated to admit it, but he was still missing Marisol.

It had been a few months now. Previously he had come to regard her as a close companion. Yes, there had been the odd moment when she would say something endearing, or they would just be talking and find themselves gazing a little too long into each other's eyes. But he had dismissed it at the time as friendly affection.

But now he realised there could be something more between himself and Marisol than just friendship.

He had been missing her much more than he thought he would. But, from their most recent conversation, he got the feeling that she may not be coming back any time soon.

He decided he should at least send her a text and see how things were going in Madrid.

He finished putting the breakfast dishes into the dishwasher and sat down in the big wicker chair near the patio doors, popped on his reading glasses, and began to write the text.

He was agonising over how to start. Should it be a simple *Hi?* No, too casual. *Hola?* No, too patronising. *Dear Marisol?* No, too formal. He stared at the phone in his hand and waited for inspiration.

Just then the thing rang loudly and made him jump. He almost dropped it onto the tiled floor where it would not have come off well (like the last time).

He recognised the number in the caller display. It was Inspector Juan. His shock was replaced by anticipation – coupled with the relief of putting off writing the text.

He answered and Juan excitedly ran his theory by him.

Frank listened carefully and nodded firmly. Yes, he concurred, it did sound like the Mozambique Drill alright. He went over the progeny of the term so they could both be sure they were talking about the same thing.

 It was a phrase originally coined by the Mozambique Militia and used to train snipers in what was called 'reflexive shooting'. Ensuring a certain kill by shooting bullets in a formation of 2 to the chest and 1 to the head. The technique became widespread and was used with variations, to train military snipers in armed forces all around the world.

Juan was elated that he had called it right.

'So.' Said Frank 'We are looking for somone ex-military. You should check those witnesses again for any ex-servicemen. Anyone who returned from active service, perhaps in the infantry. Maybe someone who had problems. Check with the Army Veterans Support Association as they keep good records. You are looking for someone who also might have an personal axe to grind against the Mayor.'

'I'll get right on it and update you.' Juan slipped the phone into his pocket and began whistling happily as he jogged back to his car.

He was like a schoolboy with a new puppy. Now they had a lead. Now they had a shot at catching the Fiesta Killer before he struck again. Now all he had to do was track down a ruthless and well-trained Killer.

'A GOOD MAN WITH A GUN'

Manuel Garcia sat on the front porch of his house nursing a glass of whisky, a loaded rifle across his lap. Today was the day and he was ready for them.

A sudden flutter of movement caught his eye as a Hoopoe landed on the lawn of his garden. He smiled. It was the same one that kept coming back time after time.

He had never had any inclination to take a shot at it. He was a good man with a gun, who had shot other men, but he had never thought of shooting a bird or an animal. The thought horrified him. Not like so many of the others in his Army unit who had delighted in using the local Afghan wildlife for target practice.

It had been nearly four years since he had been invalided out of the Armed Forces and returned home to Menorca.

Yet the memories of serving in that far flung fly-blown hellhole seemed as fresh as yesterday. If he thought about it for any length of time, it became all too real.

The acrid smells, the loud sounds, oppressive heat and the constant clouds of flies. But the worst part was the faces that came when he closed his eyes. They were the faces of his fallen comrades. His brothers and sisters in arms. They haunted his days and nights. On the rare occasions that he managed to get to sleep, after heavily self-medicating, they haunted his dreams.

Some had been killed in firefights. Some in rocket attacks on their camp. Some lost to IED's when on patrol. Those like him, who did return home, still bore the scars. Mental and physical. Open wounds that refused to heal.

Rastorno por estrés postraumático (Post Traumatic Stress Disorder) it said on his discharge papers. It entitled him to a small pension and weekly Veterans counselling sessions, but nothing seemed to help.

Then, after 7 months of therapy, he decided to try and get his life back on track. He'd always fancied setting up in business as a builder, just like his late father whose small building business had been well-known and favoured by many in the Ciutadella area.

He had helped out on many occasions as a boy, and a young man before joining the army, and he had learned a great deal about construction methods and running a small business. He continued his builder's apprenticeship in the Army and succeeded in becoming qualified before his unit was shipped overseas to Afghanistan - where there was still a lot of insurgent fighting and unrest.

He borrowed heavily from a bank to set up his business. He secured a loan against his house, the family home he had inherited. It was a gamble, but he didn't see that he had much choice.

It was hard going for the first year and a half, and at times he thought he would go under from lack of business. But after completing a few small projects, the word got around just how good and reliable his company was, and things started taking off.

By the end of the second year he was almost having to turn business away. He had a permanent workforce of 8 and contracted in bricklayers, plumbers, electricians and other tradesmen as needed, to scale up for each project.

Business was doing well, and in the summer of the next year he hit the jackpot. A prestigious council contract for a brand new retirement complex at Cala Blanca of 27 purpose-built properties for the elderly.

He put in a tender but didn't really think he had a serious chance of getting it. It was the biggest he had ever pitched for and the most expensive in terms of outlay, and he was up against some serious contenders with deeper pockets.

But he considered it was worth the risk, as the profits would not only enable him to expand his operation, but also to keep him trading for many years. So he put in a very competitive bid.

He was amazed and delighted when his firm was awarded the contract. Such a prestigious project in his portfolio would also put his firm in the top tier for similar sized tenders.

There was a gamble involved of course, as it now meant even more borrowing to pay for the contractors and materials up front, which was always a requirement with projects of this scale. But he reasoned it was a calculated risk, as the project was from a very reliable source, after all. Enough to reassure his suppliers and satisfy the bank that he was a solid bet. And as soon as the contract was won, he took out a large second mortgage.

He wasn't too worried. He knew that council projects rarely got cancelled once they were underway. That only happened with dodgy private investor groups in the bad old days of boom and bust, when everyone was jumping on the holiday property bandwagon.

No. A council contract these days was as good as gold. That's why you didn't need to take out expensive insurance indemnities against sudden curtailment. You were advised to, but in this case it seemed an unnecessary expense.

Why throw away extra money, he reasoned, when it was such a sure thing?

At last. The bad dreams were receding. Good times were on the horizon. Everything in the Garcia garden was looking rosy. He wished he still had a partner to share it with, but Chico had left in the days when life with Manuel had been unbearable.

Chico was a lovely, considerate and easy-going man. But try as he did to help Manuel adjust back to civilian life, in the end - with the sudden outbursts of temper, with the nightmares and the tears, and when the drinking had got the better of Manuel, there was no living with him.

The more Manuel drank the worse he became and in the end Chico, the love of his life, left him.

But that was all in the past. Now that dame fortune had at last smiled upon him, it was time to start again. To face the demons down and embrace a bright new future.

The prestigious project opened a lot of doors, and he was also able to secure a lot of credit lines with large companies for things like cement, cranes, diggers and other expensive heavy plant required.

They broke ground in September. The Mayor himself was there for the official ceremony and said a few words on behalf of the council. It was all over the papers and the local evening news. By November they had the foundations, footings and major services in place. Everything was ready for the building phase.

Then the bad news came.

The letter he got from the council claimed that he had failed to take out the necessary insurance securities and therefore had to forfeit.

He couldn't believe it. While it was true that he had failed to take *every* fiscal precaution, he knew from experience that this was a formality. It should now be a simple matter of filing for the necessary certificates in retrospect.

He knew it. Every builder worth his salt knew it. It was just a matter of crossing I's and dotting T's surely?

Manuel suspected there was more to it than a simple omission in his paperwork. Especially when he heard that the project was already being awarded to another local building firm. The one that happened to be owned by the Mayor's cousin.

Manuel's desperate pleas to the council planning department made no difference. The lawyers he consulted said that he could appeal, but that, although unprecedented in modern times, the council were within their legal rights to break contract with him and provide him with no recompense.

He was broke, busted and disgusted. He was madder than hell. It broke his heart to have to tell his crew to stop work at the site. They were a good bunch of guys who worked well together.

He knew some of them personally. A few were ex-soldiers like himself, trying to get their lives back together. Now he had to let them go. Now he had to send back all the equipment. Now he not only had to shut down the project, but with so much money owed and not a penny left to his name, he had to default and declare the business and himself bankrupt.

That shitty council and Mayor had stitched him up. They had double-crossed him! It wasn't fair. It wasn't right.

The anger had eaten away at him, day after day and night after night. When he did manage to sleep, the bad dreams came back worse than ever.

He told his troubles to his appointed trauma counsellor. But she was no real help. He hit the bottle hard once more. It helped while he was drunk, but it made things seem much worse when he was sober again.

He sat at home. The place untidy. Sink full of dishes. Staring at the TV but not really watching. Just drinking and drinking.

The mail piled up on the doormat. Bills, final demands and then one day, a letter that looked very important. The bold red letters stamped across it said 'ACT NOW. REPOSSESSION NOTICE'.

When he opened it he saw it was from his bank telling him that his mortgage payments were in such bad arrears, if he did not repay the debt in full plus interest, they would take steps to repossess his house.

He began to shake and then broke down in tears. How had it come to this? What had he done to deserve it? He had worked hard and honestly.

He had served his country and seen things no man should ever have to witness. And this is how he is treated.

That greedy council and Mayor had ruined him by stealing his business.

Someone should pay for this sin!

In his anger he picked up an empty scotch bottle and went to throw it at the TV screen. But stopped. It was showing a cloud with light radiating from beneath with golden rays falling onto the open pages of The Holy Bible. A caption beneath said *'The answer to your troubles are in here'*.

He thought it odd because he had been watching a Western on the movie channel. Then he realized he had stood on the TV remote, and by chance had tuned it to an Evangelist Christian channel.

Manuel was not a particularly religious man, but in Afghanistan he had prayed on many occasions, and he believed that someone, somewhere was listening.

He'd been praying lately. Maybe this was a sign.

Would he find the answer to his troubles in the Bible?

He ran to the bedroom and dug out the dog-eared copy of The Holy Bible he had been given by his army padre.

He quickly thumbed through the pages of the Old Testament until he found what he was looking for. Yes! There it was in Exodus. Moses: The 8th commandment: *Thou shalt not steal.*

Over the next few weeks he made his plans. He would meet out divine justice. Make an example of the Mayor where everyone could see him for the thief that he was. Easter was coming soon, and with it the perfect opportunity.

He smiled at how fitting a way it would be to make a public example of the Mayor.

He saw that the Hoopoe on the lawn had been joined by several others, all eagerly searching for insects in the grass. They scattered as several vehicles pulled up sharply in the road outside his gate.

Blue flashing lights! He was expecting the Bailiffs not the police. He had been informed that they would be coming today to evict him and secure the property.

No matter. What had to be done, had to be done.

He stood up, finished his drink and waved at the police cars. He held up the rifle to show them he meant business, then got down on his knees behind the porch rail.

Resting the rifle on the top of the rail, he couldn't but help chuckle at the irony. Here he was, a highly trained Army Marksman. A gunny. One of the best in his unit. Yet this was the easiest shot he would ever make.

Chico would have seen the joke if he had been here. His lovely precious Chico. With that thought a gentle tear rolled down his cheek.

He placed the tip of the rifle barrel against his forehead. The metal felt strangely warm for what was often called cold steel.

Somewhere in the distance he heard car doors slamming, then shouting, getting louder.

He placed his thumb on the trigger and squeezed.

'Well, that's it then. We have found The Fiesta Killer.'

Juan filled both of their glasses and handed one to Frank. He'd stopped by his place the next day to tell him the good news - that Frank had been right about it being an ex-military man with an axe to grind against the Mayor.

He told him all about Manuel Garcia. About the man's poor mental state, his business folding, the blame he apportioned to the Mayor. Sadly, he had killed himself before they could arrest him and bring him in for questioning. But the bullets dug out of the Mayor matched the unique striation marks from his rifle. They also found evidence in his house of his plans. Notes in a small diary.

It was all there. The hatred of the Mayor. Blaming him for his misfortune. His plan to kidnap the poor man and exact his revenge at the annual *Slaughter of the Rag Dolls*.

Frank listened and nodded silently.

Juan raised his glass and proposed a toast. 'Fiesta Killer, case closed!'

Frank clinked his glass half-heartedly. He seemd to be deep in thought then said 'I'm not so sure.'

Juan raised an eyebrow and looked at him quizzically. 'What? But we have all the evidence. The bullets. Pretty much a blow-by-blow confession!' Juan looked quite upset.

Frank smiled and put his hand on his friend's shoulder. 'Relax. Yes. There's no doubt that Manuel Garcia shot and killed the Mayor. You have got your man there.'

He stood and went to the open patio doors. It was shaded but you could feel the heat as soon as you crossed the threshold. Fortunately, the air-con was on full blast and took the edge off.

'I'm just not sure that he was the Fiesta Killer.'

Juan gave him a questioning look and shrugged his shoulders 'Why not? What makes you say that?'

'Well…the man was disturbed right enough. He had a strong motive for killing the Mayor. He blamed him for ruining his business. It was a crime of passion. Revenge. It was personal.'

He turned and paced slowly around the room as he went on. 'But he had no reason to kill any of the others at the Fiestas.

I mean why would he? He'd had his revenge and there was no mention in his diary of carrying on. There was no reason for him to do so. He had nothing personal against *them*. So it doesn't make any sense.'

Also, you say he was clean shaven and there was no sign of a red cap or combat jacket around his place.

Juan was silent as he thought about this. Yes, he could see the logic of Frank's argument, but he was not really convinced. 'Okay. Let's say you are right. But if he didn't do the other murders, then who did, and why?'

Frank stopped his pacing and sat down on the armchair. 'I thought from the start there was something we were missing. Almost as if someone was playing a game with us. It was all a bit too precise and calculated. I had a feeling that I'd seen it all before somewhere.'

'Then I remembered a case back in the UK. In Brighton back in the 80's. There was a brutal murder there. A woman's body was found on the beach one morning. She'd been killed in the most…' Here he winced as he recalled the horrible details of the crime scene. Ritualistic markings all over the body and weird symbols like Egyptian glyphs drawn in the wet sand. There was also some…'

He shook off the gory image and continued. 'Well let's just say it was very strange. We caught the killer. He confessed and told us that Alien voices had made him do it. They had been speaking to him through his radio, telling him to help them harvest human organs. To kill and prepare the victims and leave them on the beach to be beamed up at night.'

Juan looked visibly shocked. 'Yuk! That is disgusting and very crazy!'

'Yes. It was in all the papers for weeks. When they caught him, they put him away in a psych unit for a long spell.'

Juan laughed darkly. 'I should hope so!'

Frank smiled sadly and shook his head as he went on with his recollection. 'Yes. But a few months later, when he was safely locked away, the killings started up again. Same sick ritual. Same glyphs drawn in the sand.'

'Yes. There could only be one answer for that my friend. And I think that is what is going on here.'

Frank was silent for a while as he waited for Juan to process this. By the sudden change in the policeman's expression he could tell that he had come to the same conclusion.

Juan nodded in agreement and said 'A Copycat.'

LA FIESTA DEL VERGE DE GRÀCIA
'DEAD RECKONING'

The Fiesta Del Verge De Gracia of Mahon in September is the highlight of the Menorcan Fiesta Calendar.

It's the big one. It takes place throughout the town with the main focus being the Harbour area, and it draws in the largest crowds and the biggest parades. It also has the grandest fireworks display. A pyrotechnic extravaganza that starts at the stroke of midnight on the last day.

As the moment approaches, crowds of people gather on the hillsides overlooking the harbour. At a given signal, all the town lights in the area are switched off. With ten seconds to go, the crowd counts down to the stroke of midnight and then the fiery show begins.

It goes on for some 20 minutes and finishes with the spectacular Underwater Fireworks, where large display rockets shoot up from under the water in the middle of the Harbour and explode with a Kaleidoscope of colours in the night skies above the darkened capital.

Every year, a visiting dignitary or celebrity is invited to start the proceedings by giving a short speech and ceremoniously pulling a lever. Sometimes it is a well-known TV personality. Sometimes a famous footballer. Sometimes a visiting politician or even a royal.

Chief Inspector Magda Helena Volterra stood in front of the dozen officers she had assembled in the briefing room.

There was a map on the wall of Mahon Harbour with areas circled in red marker. Juan assumed it was key areas of the Fiesta, and now that his shoulder was healing nicely he was ready for active duty.

'This is a plain clothes and low-key operation. Understood?' The Chief eyed them sternly.

All nodded. She continued 'The Serbian Cultural Attaché will be guest of honour at the Mahon Fiesta. He will be launching the proceedings.' She looked around the room slowly as if expecting a question.

None came and she carried on.

'As you know, we have caught the Fiesta Killer, but according to *some...* ' Here she gave Juan a sarcastic look, then continued '...there could still be a Copycat out there deciding to carry on where the Fiesta Killer left off. So, unlikely though that is in my opinion, we must remain vigilant. So be on the lookout for Señor Red Cap. Or in this case his twin brother!' She smiled at her joke but no one laughed.

She turned to the map on the wall and used a long pointer. 'I want men to be stationed here, here and here.'

'This Fiesta being the main Fiesta of the year might just bring out the psycho in someone. The profiler says that they crave attention.'

Juan asked. 'So, what's the plan Chief?'

'Good question officer Rodreguez.' She turned again to the map and using the pointer said 'You will split into three main details. I will be chief liaison officer, stationed in the command module, of course.' They all nodded and murmured.

'We'll need officer Diaz and his group to watch the perimeter here, and here.' She tapped on the map showing the main routes down to the Harbour. 'And officer... Flores? He held up his hand. 'You and the other officers in your group will infiltrate the crowd along the parade route.'

She looked once more at Juan.

'Officer Rodreguez?'

'Yes Chief?'

'I want you and your men to handle a special protective detail on the podium.'

'Yes Chief.'

She used the pointer once more indicating an area just at the waterfront where a floating platform had been specially constructed for the occasion. It seemed to be jutting out quite far into the water.

'You and your men will take up position here, and here. I've asked Weapons and Tactical to issue you with appropriate body armour and firearms.'

Juan raised his eyebrows and tilted his head in a questioning manner. Firearms were not his strong suit. Yes, he had used a weapon and killed in the line of duty. But he considered it a last resort and one to be avoided if possible.

She caught his concerned look. 'It will be your job to protect the Serbian Cultural Attaché. We can't afford to take risks. So, if any son of a bitch tries anything, red, blue or sunset yellow cap, you are fully authorized to use any necessary force to take him out of the game.'

There was a sudden buzz in the room. 'Any necessary force!' No police officer had discharged a weapon outside of the firing range in the last five years! Save of course that incident with the wild boar up at Punta Grossa last Spring. The poor creature turned out to be a muddy pig that had escaped from a farm there.

Still. Perhaps this was no surprise. The new Chief was very keen on firearms. She had made weekly weapons training compulsory, and her office wall displayed many certificates she had been awarded for her expertise. A brief stint as a sniper with SWAT was the pride of her CV and, with a few successful hostage incidents, she had earned the nickname of 'Crack Shot' Volterra.

Juan chuckled recalling this. Then the smile vanished from his lips. If Frank was right, the Fiesta Killer Copycat was out there, and he was being asked, no ordered, to put himself and his men in the line of fire.

The road down to the Harbour, the Costa de ses Voltes, weaved like some giant angular snake. It reminded Juan of world-famous Lombard Street in San Francisco, with its eight hairpin bends. This road was on a much smaller scale and nowhere nearly as long or the hill as steep. There were just five hairpin bends, one at the end of each 100 feet or so of straight pathway.

Between the paths were large grassed areas dotted with flowerbeds, succulents and tall palm and pine trees. Today these areas were thronged with people, packed alongside the path edges, all waiting for the big parade to start.

The crowd was abuzz with anticipation and excitement. The grown-ups chatting and laughing. Small children squealing with delight playing hide and seek amongst the legs of the adults. Teenagers shouting, goofing around and guzzling large amounts of Pomada.

It seemed as if the whole of Menorca had turned out to watch the show. Not many wanted to miss this prime annual event. This peerless celebration of Menorcan culture and spirit. The initial highlight of which was the arrival of the Gigantes.

Juan stood at the bottom of the hill, just where the pathway met the port road junction. It was a small semi-circular concreted area with wide steps leading down from the zigzag path.

The crowd was kept behind tape barriers, not that it stopped youngsters from crawling underneath. Neither did it stop the occasional drunken teenager from dashing out to perform dancing or mooning, with the raucous encouragement of his friends.

He and his men, discreetly positioned up and down the hill, carefully checked for any odd behavior or suspicious looking characters. Gigantes excepted.

Not an easy task amongst this lively, jostling melee.

His men were on edge. The crowd not so, blissfully unaware of any danger. A potential killer in their midst.

He scanned the crowd. The light now fading from an evening flat white to a pink tinged soft smoke. There! Two rows up! A red baseball cap! A man with a beard. He was pointing something! A gun? It was hard to see, but there was no time to take any chances.

Before he could alert his men, the figure disappeared in a crowd of bodies. Officers suddenly seemed to pour out from the crowd like bees from a hive poked with a stick. Clearly, they had already spotted the suspect and the word had gone out to take him down.

A yell. A scream. More shouts as the officers descended on the man in the red cap. They brought him to the ground like hounds on a deer.

The crowd parted in shock. Juan arrived, gun drawn and yelling at the people to keep back. He saw that his officers had successfully subdued the assassin, now sat on the ground, head down and hands cuffed behind him.

He reached down and removed the red cap to reveal the face of a tearful young teenage girl. A false, stick-on beard now hanging by some tape from her chin.

The 'Gun' beside her on the floor was nothing more than a selfie stick with a mobile phone still in place on the far end.

He picked up the cap and could see that it was much like the one the killer wore in the video. He gently removed the fake beard. This was just a young girl here for fun and partying like everyone else. This was not the assassin. But why the red cap and stick-on facial hair? Was it just a coincidence?

He had her hands uncuffed and gently helped her to her feet. She just stood there sobbing a little, sniffling and wiping her eyes, still shocked and clearly upset by the whole thing. Juan gave her his handkerchief and a reassuring smile and apologized on behalf of his men.

He explained that they had been warned about troublemakers and this was a case of mistaken identity. That went a long way to placate her, not least because of Juan's very acceptable bedside manner. Even for a man in his late forties, he was still handsome and seemed to have a special charm with women of all ages. He enquired about the red cap and the fake beard.

The girl seemed embarrassed at this. With shaking voice she said that it was all part of a 'Crowd Event', a challenge sent out on Social Media to come to the Fiesta wearing a red baseball cap and a false beard, and that you could claim a 50 Euro prize if you posted your selfie online.

Juan called off his men and apologized to the young girl once more. She returned to her friends in the crowd somewhat shaken, but would soon be back in the spirit of things after several more drinks.

The word went around that all was okay. Everyone on watch breathed a sigh of relief. Juan spread the unsettling news that there may be a few more red-capped and selfie stick wielding young people in the crowd tonight, and to proceed carefully next time.

He shook his head at the prospect. A bit of fun? Or was it the 'Copycat' Killer trying to muddy the waters?

'Here they come!' Someone shouted.

A brass band struck up and a shiver of excitement ran through the crowd. Heads all turned toward the top of the hill like a slow murmuration as the parade approached.

Cheers went up as the first float arrived, surrounded by marching adventure scouts. On it was a tableau of a Hawaiian island scene, complete with fake coconut trees, 'Apes' and dancers in grass skirts.

This was followed by a host of more 'Paradise Island' themed floats, plus lorries and vans advertising local businesses gaily adorned with festive accessories. The crowd were delighted by the many sporting and rotary clubs, schools and other groups in fancy dress, and the many uniformed bands and orchestras piping, drumming and twirling batons to the music.

Juan stood clapping and smiling. It reminded him so much of similar parades he had seen during his childhood in Madrid. True, some of the floats were bigger and more professional looking there. And the scale of the whole parade much grander. But here, there was such a wonderful sense of togetherness. Of family, that one can only feel by being part of a close-knit community with a shared ancestry.

It was reaffirming and made Juan feel at home and like an interloper at the same time.

As the last of the pipers passed by, he heard a new buzz from the top of the hill. He looked up but had to stretch to see above the crowd. He just managed to catch a glimpse of the top of a big brown shiny head. A head as big as a garden shed bobbing up and down as the parade moved forward.

'Look!' Someone cried 'Here come the Gigantes. It's the Alcalde himself I think!' Much laughter rang through the crowd.

But Juan wasn't laughing. He had the growing uneasy feeling that the Fiesta Killer was alive and well and planning something big.

And that this night would end badly for someone.

By 11pm there had been 14 red capped and fake bearded individuals stopped and questioned. Most had been spotted on CCTV. The police had feeds from all the cameras in the harbour area routed to their on-site command post - a large panel sided truck parked on a hilltop overlooking the harbour.

Each person they stopped had the same story. A call to action on a website: Red cap, beard and take a selfie. Post it online and make 50 euros.

It was a frustrating evening and it caused a lot of unnecessary work for the Mahon Police. Juan suspected that was the intention. A diversionary tactic intended to keep them all busy while the real 'Fiesta Killer' conducted yet another murder of biblical retribution.

But who would the victim be this time?

He ran all this through his brain as he made his way along the harbour road, the Moll de Llevant, to the specially constructed jetty where the VIP would ceremoniously start the Fireworks display.

The VIP! The Serbian Cultural Attaché. Was he the intended victim of the Copycat? Unlikely. So far the Killer had targeted only Menorcan folk. Still, it *was* possible.

But when he arrived at the Jetty and saw just how tight the security measures were, he thought otherwise. For one thing, in addition to the barriers manned by burly and well-armed officers at the entrance gates, there was only one way on and off this small pier-like structure.

Then there was about 100 feet of planked walkway with railings on either side, and a straight drop of about 8 meters to the water. No easy access there.

The whole thing was supported by a criss-crossing network of steel beams that ran underneath the entire length of the structure. Anyone trying to gain entry that way by climbing would be quickly and easily seen.

He showed his badge to the men at the gate who let him through. It was purely protocol as the men were his own officers, but it was instilled in them to follow procedure.

As he neared the large circular platform at the end of the 'pier' he was quite impressed. Not with all the Fiesta frippery that sparkled or winked in the fading light. But to the one side of the dias on which the 'launch' ceremony would be taking place, was a very sophisticated looking array of screens and control panels.

To Juan it looked like a scaled down version of NASA mission control. There were banks of switches and levers and blinking lights. Many had hand-written or printed labels stuck on them. On closer inspection Juan could see that they were control switches for the firework display, lasers, and music. This was the place from where the entire show would be conducted.

He stood near the centre of the platform and looked all around. Out in front, across the stretch of dark water to Cala Llonga, some half a mile away he could see feint lights from houses and streetlamps on its hills.

Torch lights flickered and flashed from the island in the middle of the Harbour where people were readying the rockets.

The wind was favourable. Just a few Km per hour. It was a warm September night, but nothing exceptional for this time of the year. So, conditions were ideal for a safe launch.

On the platform some technicians were busying themselves checking controls, twiddling knobs and talking into headphone microphones. Watching them work he got quite mesmerised, until a familiar voice from behind made him jump.

'It's all controlled by computer lad! There's nowt to worry about.'

Charlie! Who else? He had waxed lyrical to Juan about the display Fireworks, particularly the underwater variety. Juan, being quite new to the island had yet to see them. And, of course, who else but Charlie would be here as a VIP guest on this most special night?

He turned and shook Charlie's hand warmly.

'Señor MacKay. Good to see you again.'

'*Charlie*, please. What brings you here Lad? Looking for that copycat Fiesta Killer eh?'

Juan was not too surprised that Charlie knew all about the Copycat. He knew everything that happened in Menorca. He realised he would probably have talked to Frank who would have shared his doubts about Manuel Garcia being responsible for all the Fiesta murders.

Juan shrugged 'Well, you cannot be too careful.'

Charlie shook his head and made a concerned face 'Aye.' He pointed to his own temple. 'That lad' had something loose up here. Plenty more of them about I reckon.'

Juan nodded. 'That is for sure. So, we must take every precaution tonight.'

Charlie looked around at the heavy security presence. There were men with metal detectors walking among the 20 or so chairs set in rows for the VIP guests.

'Aye. Well y'seem to have it all in hand, so I'll just nip off for a wee dram and be back at midnight for the big switch on.'

With a smile and backward wave Charlie departed.

Satisfied that all was in order, Juan decided to make his way off the platform and return later too. Just before he left, he couldn't help noticing the big red button at the top of the Mission Control desk. It had the word 'SUBMARINA' written in large red letters just below it.

The urge to go over and press it was almost overwhelming.

MIDNIGHT FIREWORKS

The first thing Frank Harmer noticed was the smell of cigarette smoke. He also felt cold. He opened his eyes and found he was in a darkened room. It was hard to see anything. Where was he? Was the room moving or was it him? His head hurt and it was difficult to focus his thoughts.

Then his mind began to clear and his short-term memory started to return.

Yes. He had been in Irina's Hotel room. He had gone there to take her to the Fiesta. The idea was to have a quick drink in the hotel bar and then head down to the Harbour to catch the Parade.

This was going to be her final night in Menorca. The Serbian Opera Company were moving on to Sardinia, the next stop on their tour. So, this would be a bittersweet night for them both.

He had grown very fond of Irina and did not want to say

goodbye. In spite of her mercurial personality - her sudden shifts between dismissive coldness and warm, almost childlike tenderness - he felt they had a connection.

Although she insisted that she was not interested in a long-term relationship, there was still something there.

He had got assurances from Irina that Goran would be otherwise engaged this evening, partying somewhere with the rest of the troupe. So they could both enjoy this last night together without the large, evil-humoured 'gooseberry' in tow.

Frank had enquired at the Hotel desk, and was told she had left instructions for him go up to her room and wait for her. The receptionist also informed him that she was at the hairdressers and was running late. He'd taken the lift and used a Key Card given to him by the receptionist to enter her room.

It was one of the grander rooms of the 4 Star residence. The simple yet stylish cream and gold décor. The intricate lacework on the pretty cotton bedcover. A large built-in double wardrobe. En-suite with spa bath. Fresh fruit. Chilled Drinks cabinet.

It also had a fine view over the town rooftops all the way down to the port, with the Hills of Cala Llonga on the other side of the water, now painted in a soft golden burnish by the last rays of the setting sun.

Next… what happened next? He struggled to recall as the lumpy fog cleared slowly in his brain. Ah yes. He'd sat in that comfy-looking leather tub chair…switched on the TV… leafed through a complementary tourist magazine entitled 'in2menorca' (very popular on the island). And, getting bored after half an hour, he'd decided to take a quick peek inside the capacious built-in double wardrobe.

Gorgeous gowns and fabulous frocks of all shades and materials were hung there. Knowing the kind of woman Irina was, he had expected there to be some nice clothes, but even he was surprised by the myriad of magnificent outfits hanging side-by-side filling the entire closet rail.

On the shelf above sat many hats, gloves and bags. Accessories for all occasions. He'd suddenly had an urge to try a hat on. After all, there was no-one else around. He'd reached up and taken down a brown Fedora, put it on his head, tilted it to one side and, in the tall door mirror did his best Humphrey Bogart impression.

'Here's lookin at you Kid.'

He thought his Bogie was rubbish. He laughed and went to put the hat back where it lived, dropped it on the floor of the closet and bent to pick it up. It was then he had noticed the case. On the floor at the back under the hanging clothes. A battered looking, black guitar case. It had travel stickers all over the lid and sides.

He'd thought it odd. Not the fact that she had travelled a lot, but that she had lugged the thing around with her when she could not play. She had told him over a drink one evening that, although she was a gifted singer with a 4 Octave range, she couldn't play a note on any musical instrument.

They had both found it hilarious at the time.

Of course! He had concluded. It must belong to Goran. The man had fingers like hotdog sausages, but he may well have been able to play a few tunes, albeit badly. Yes. That had to be it.

Curious, he'd bent down and flipped the catches and opened the case. What he saw inside had puzzled and shocked him. No guitar. Just some maps neatly folded, some kind of hand-held gaming controller, some Ray-Ban sunglasses, and the things that shocked him the most, a fake beard and… a red baseball cap!

His hands were shaking as he reached into the case and fished it out. He'd held it up and turned it around, examining it. Surely not? There had to be a simple explanation. Pure coincidence?

With his mind racing, he had unfolded one of the maps on the floor. It was a map of Menorca. In red felt pen, areas were clearly marked out at different locations. There were hand-written notes, dates, names and numbers.

He had quickly realised that they all corresponded to the times and locations and identities of the victims, and the numbers found at each of the Fiesta Murders. All with the exception of the Mayor's bizarre murder.'

It was hard to believe, but the evidence here was also hard to ignore. Was Goran the true Fiesta Killer?

Frank never got to answer the question. He hadn't heard someone enter the room, nor pick up a small statuette of a rearing Menorcan horse from the coffee table. The sound from the TV would have masked that. All he knew was a sudden searing pain in the back of his skull and then darkness.

At 11.29 Juan Diego Rodriguez, Inspector Jefe of the Mahon Police stood on the Dias, checked his watch and surveyed the scene. Slowly and carefully he checked the walkway leading to the ceremonial platform where the Serbian Cultural Attaché would be starting the fireworks display.

Any minute now the party of city councillors and other bigwigs would be making their way along the walkway to take their seats. He could see a gaggle of press photographers assembled at the barrier, policed by heavily armed guards from the Guardia Civil.

His own men were positioned with him here among the guest seating area, and around the perimeter of the Dias.

Little lights winked all over the Mahon Harbour hillside from homes, hotels and streetlamps. Their orange reflections bounced along the ripples of dark water and stretched out towards him in random broken gold leaf.

His earpiece suddenly crackled into life. The delegation had arrived. No sign of anything suspicious. The green light was given and the VIP party began to approach, walking and chatting happily along the boardwalk.

His men took their ready positions. The group arrived at the Dias and began taking their seats. The guest of honour - the Attaché - a large man in a grey suit wearing a pink Peony in his lapel, was seated next to the Mayor of Mahon. They were at the front just a few steps away from the rostrum and the ceremonial 'start' lever which was festooned with ribbons and a big red bow.

The device had no practical function. It was just for show and not connected to the electronic network that would set all the evening fireworks in motion, and keep them operating in sequence. It was purely for visual and ceremonial effect.

The *real* show would be started by the guy sat lower down and to the right of the Dias at the control consul, the one with the nice big red button at the top marked *Underwater Fireworks*. These display rockets – the finale of the show - would be launched from silos submerged beneath the water in the middle of the harbour channel.

They were always the biggest and most spectacular bangs. So big that the lightshow could even be seen from Mallorca, some 20 miles across the sea.

Minutes ticked by as the Mayor stood and made a welcoming speech. Followed by a leading local Politician and then someone from the Menorca Arts and Culture Society. Sounds of music and merriment drifted occasionally across the water, punctuating the night air and filling in any pauses in the speeches.

A warm breeze and a starry sky promised perfect viewing conditions for the display.

All the invited guests seemed to be here. Everything appeared to be going well.

He spotted Charlie Mack seated near the front and gave him a nod. Charlie looked around theatrically, stretched out his arms and indicted the empty seats next to him, then shrugged.

Juan suddenly realised what he was getting at. Where was Señor Frank and his special guest Irina Perkaz?

Juan shook his head and shrugged back at him. He hoped they would make it before the fireworks started.

Now the fog had cleared in Frank's head. He was in the cabin of a Yacht. A fancy one, like Charlie's. Out through the windows it was pitch black, but he could feel the swaying motion and hear the gentle hum of a motor.

He was sat at a table on a metal frame dining chair. He tried to move but his hands were bound together at the wrists and his feet were tied to the legs of the chair. His vision adjusted to the dim cabin light and he saw her. Sat opposite, just staring at him.

'Irina?' His voice came out as a croak.

She smiled thinly and said 'Good. You are alive. I was worried Goran had hit you too hard and killed you!'

She got up and came over to him. She took a large drag from her cigarette and blew a huge cloud of smoke into the air.

Frank was still confused. 'Irina. What the hell is going on? Why am I tied to this chair? How did I get here?'

'Goran and I 'helped' you. We carried you between us. I could not risk leaving you there to wreck my plans. So, we propped you up like a drunk. You were my old uncle who had too much Pomada. Easy to believe on such a festive occasion. You would not be the only one I think.'

He did not know what hurt the worst. His head, or the fact that he was her 'old' Uncle. He assumed that Goran was now driving this boat.

She looked at her watch and said impatiently 'Please make the next question short as I have to get to work. In about five minutes I shall be terminating the life of the Serbian

Cultural Attaché. '

'You…what?'

She sighed heavily and shook her head. 'What? Is it so difficult to believe? That I am a ruthless assassin? Your red cap wearing Fiesta Killer? She placed a length of her own hair under her nose to make a joke moustache.

The pieces of the jigsaw began to finally fit into place. The items in the guitar case weren't Goran's. They were hers!

Yet there were so many other things that didn't make sense.

'But you… I mean, why?'

She tilted her head back and let out a derisory laugh and said. '*Why*?' I shall tell you a story. A short story, as I have to get on. But I *would* like you to know why. I think I owe you that for pleasant company. You have been a welcome distraction and an excellent source of information.' Here she leaned forward and blew him a kiss. 'And besides, I really do like you.'

She sat down opposite him at the table. Her face became serious. 'When I was a young girl, the Serbians came into our town, searching they said for Terrorists.'

'Wait a minute, aren't *you* Serbian?'

A hot look filled her eyes and she spat on the floor. Serbian! I am no stinking Serbian. I am Kosovan Alabanian born and raised. Well, at least until Milosevic's soldiers came and took my parents away. They tortured them. Made them confess to terrible crimes they did not commit and then had them shot as Terrorists. The lying shit pigs!'

Now he saw hatred and tears in her eyes. He was moved and said.'Irina. That is awful.'

She looked away into the distance and into the past. 'After, they took me to Belgrade and placed me in a camp for…' She glanced at her watch again. 'Well, eventually I was taken in by a nice and quite wealthy Serbian family. My new Father was an Officer in the Serbian Army. My new mother a seamstress for the Opera. My Father taught me to hunt and shoot a rifle, and my new Mother spotted my talent for singing and got me an introduction to the Opera.'

She looked back at him, wiped her eyes and glanced once more at her watch and said.' There is a lot more to my story but to cut it short, as you say, I have a score to settle. The Serbian Cultural Attaché is one Rudnik Pavkovic. He was one of the Officers that rounded up my parents and others who were fighting for the Kosovo Liberation Army. He gave the orders to have them and all their families shot. The women and the old folk and the little…'

Her eyes went cold. 'He spared my life.' She placed a hand on her stomach and said bitterly 'For a price.'

Frank realised what she was getting at and, despite his dire situation, his heart went out to her. She saw his look of pity but shot back a look of contempt. 'I don't need your sympathy. Where was the UN? Where were the British when we needed your help? You all sat on your hands and let the bloody Serbian Army massacre our people.'

'We did send our peace keeping forces into Kosovo as I remember.' Frank offered.

'Too late!' She spat.

She took another drag of her cigarette then stubbed it out

savagely as she said. 'I swore that pig would pay. This has been a long time in the planning, and tonight my loved ones will be avenged and can rest in peace.'

Frank nodded slowly as he took this all in. Yes, he could understand her motives. He clearly remembered the TV footage in the 90's of the tanks rolling into Kosovan towns and villages, and the bloody battles that took place as they hunted down the KLA rebels.

But that did not explain everything. The wound on his skull throbbed. He felt himself swooning and heard a ringing in his ears. He shook his head clear. 'But what about the Fiesta killings? The Bible numbers. Where does all *that* fit in?'

She laughed and clapped her hands together in glee. 'Hah! It doesn't! That was all a... a crazy Goose chase. Red Herrings to lead you and the police up the garden paths. I borrowed some ideas from the movies. I added the red hat and the beard to create my character, a villain you could spot in the crowd.'

'Okay. But I still don't see why?'

She raised her eyebrows and spoke as if explaining something to a small child. 'There are two reasons. One is so you would all be looking in the wrong direction and barking up the wrong trees, as I am sure they will be doing tonight. Leaving me free to make my move. And then make my get away.'

Frank nodded 'Makes sense I guess. And the second reason?'

Here she got up and did a little dance. She threw her arms wide and sang. 'Because it was so much FUN darling!'

She stopped suddenly as she noticed the time. 'Oh dear. Time to go. Like Cinderella I must be where I need to be by Midnight. Or it will all come crashing down. Or should I say it won't!'

He needed to stall for time. Perhaps talk her out of it, although he doubted that would be possible. But it might give him time to work his bonds free and stop her. He fired another question as she headed for the door.

'What about the Mayor? I mean that was a bit obvious wasn't it. That had to be the work of a trained marksman.'

She stopped, laughed and said. 'Ah yes. The Mozambique Drill. How very clever of you to notice that. But that was not me of course. That was poor Mario Garvia or whatever his name was. But it did give me the idea.'

'What? To copy his biblical revenge note and create the illusion that we had a crazed serial killer on our hands?'

'Exactly. Goran helped me of course. He took care of the more *unpleasant* stuff. At times, I admit he did get a little carried away in his work. He may be weak in the head, but he has a very strong stomach.'

She walked over to him and stroked his hair. 'You would make a great detective, if you were going to live longer, my darling.' He winced as she touched his head wound, now covered in dried blood.

'Oh. I am sorry my sweet. Does it hurt?'

He smiled thinly and said 'Only when I think.' His head began to swim again and he fought to stop blacking out.

She started for the door once more. He *had* to stop her.

'The Fireworks!' he shouted. 'At midnight. That's to cover the sound of the shots? I suppose you think no-one is going to hear anything with all those bangs.'

She stopped, turned and smiled impishly. 'Shots? There will be no shots, my darling. There will be no rifle. Too unreliable. I have had a better idea. One that will make his death a certainty.'

She made a comical sad face and said in a child-like voice 'Unfortunately, it will mean there will be other casualties.'

Her look changed to one of hate as she added with bitterness. '*Collateral Damage* as they say in the Serbian Military.'

She softened slightly as she could see he still looked puzzled. Enjoying the game she simply added ' But it will be... spectacular.' Here she made an exploding firework gesture with her hands.

He nodded as if he was listening while, just out of view beneath the table, he busied his hands on the nylon rope that bounds his wrists. The knot had some play in it and he felt that it might come loose enough to free his hands. Whoever had tied this had clearly never been in the boy scouts. Goran no doubt.

She blew him another kiss and said 'Now I really must go. Don't worry, when I have finished, you and I and Goran will be going for a little boat ride. Unfortunately my darling, not all of us will be coming back.'

He had to stall her 'What do you mean by...'

Ignoring this, she blew him a farewell kiss and said 'Goodbye my sweet.' Then left through the door that led up the steps to the rear deck of the boat.

Goran brought the Yacht to a standstill just outside the cordoned off area of the channel. Marked with buoys and flags, this area, about a quarter of a mile from the main Harbour, had been set up to ensure no craft would get too close to the fireworks and risk an accident during the display. This had happened in the past with tragic consequences.

Only a few boats bothered to anchor mid-channel anyway as the display could easily be seen and enjoyed from the quayside moorings on either side of the Harbour.

He had turned the boat, as instructed, so that the aft deck was facing the town and all the action.

At 11.59 house lights were switched off. Garden lamps extinguished. Streetlights dimmed to a minimum. Save but the stars, cigarette ends, and mobile phones like so many glow worms, the entire Mahon Harbour was in darkness.

The hilltops overlooking the estuary were lined with thousands of people. As was the harbour road below, rooftops, verandas, and anywhere where there was a good viewing point. It appeared that the entire population of Menorca had turned out to witness this once a year spectacle.

A sotto hush went around the crowds, punctuated only by excited chatter and drunken laughter.

At 11.59 and 30 seconds the Drone was launched.

Under the cover of darkness, no one noticed as it sped down the estuary towards its target, with several pounds of high explosive packed into a metal cylinder under its gravitational centre.

It flew at a height of some 10 meters above the surface of the water. Not simply to avoid detection. The fact that it was black in colour and the surface material a dull plastic took care of that. It was just at the right height to crash into the VIP's platform without too much course correction.

This had all been carefully worked out by the operator, now viewing the Drone's progress through a VR headset with images relayed in real time from its onboard infrared camera.

So, the near total darkness was not a problem. Although, sudden flashes of highly enhanced reflections from the mast and cabin lights of the Yachts moored on either side, dazzled her eyes momentarily. Irina told herself that it had been a good decision to practice flying this amazing but tricky piece of technology on several nights during the past few weeks.

It had made her laugh to see reports in the local papers of UFO sightings.

Goran was on deck stood at the wheel, keeping the boat steady. Frank wasn't getting anywhere with the rope binding his wrists together, but suddenly realised that if he could bend forward far enough to reach the rope around his legs, which did not feel particularly tight, he could untie them. He did so and worked at the knot, even though it made his head pound and made him feel like throwing up.

At 11.59 and 50 seconds the crowds on the hillsides began to count down out loud.

'**TEN**…' No one saw the explosive laden drone closing in on its deadly destination.

'**NINE**…' No one heard the buzz of its motors.

'**EIGHT**…' No one noticed it come to a halt above the middle of the channel and hover in the air adjacent to its target.

Irina gently fingered the controls and the Drone turned slowly until the VIP platform swam into view. She pressed the Zoom and located the Serbian Cultural Attaché stood at the podium with his hand on the lever.

'**SEVEN**…' The Drone turned a little more until she had him dead centre. A huge grin split her face as she pressed the forward button once more.

'**SIX**…' Perhaps it was because Juan's senses were on high alert. Perhaps it was just dumb luck. He spotted the movement. A dark shape in the air out there above the water, about 200 yards away, moving against the background.

He was not sure at first that it wasn't a startled seabird or a bat out hunting. Then suddenly, in the pause between counts he heard the buzz of a Drone. A sound unmistakable once heard, like a swarm of angry hornets in flight. Many times he had taken his nephew to El Retiro Park and they had put one through its paces.

Some of the other guests on the platform spotted it too, but simply thought it was part of the show.

'**FIVE**…' Of course! He suddenly realised just what it was that was coming. He'd heard of similar assassination attempts using bombs by drone. He cursed himself for not thinking of it before.

'**FOUR**…' Shit! They were all going to die at the hands of the Fiesta Killer. The clever bastard was going to employ *death from above* to blow them all to kingdom come. And there was nothing he could do to stop it. Unless…

Meanwhile in the cabin, Frank had got his legs free of the rope and was heading for the door to take him up to the aft deck. There could only be a few seconds left before midnight, so there was not time to get his hands free too. He yanked it open and raced up the steps.

She was standing at the back of the deck against the rail wearing some kind of VR headset and holding the funny looking game consul thing from the guitar case. The horror of her plan and her chosen means of death delivery became clear.

An Ariel bomb, delivered by remote control.

Awful. Shocking. Brilliant.

He heard the crowds counting down in the distance.

'**THREE** …' Time was almost up. Frank knew he had to stop her before it was too late. He ran at her screaming with his arms out in front of him, his hands still tied together.

'**TWO** …' Juan shouted for everyone to take cover, and to his men to shoot at the drone. But, despite the hail of bullets, nothing seemed to be stopping it. He felt helpless, like a rabbit caught in the headlights. He looked around desperately for something, anything to protect them from the oncoming missile.

Then his gaze fell on *the big red button*.

Back on the deck of the Yacht, Irina, sensing the motion behind her, turned just in time to see the careering figure of Frank, tied arms outstretched, bearing down on her.

The words left her lips as he crashed into her. 'You are too..' She was about to say the word …'late' but his desperate momentum carried them both over the rail and into the inky black night waters.

'ONE!' Like a man possessed, Juan charged screaming at the control desk where the operator sat dumbfounded and confused by the rapidly unfolding events. He was even more surprised when Juan knocked him off his chair.

It was a slim and desperate chance, but the only one that Juan could think of trying. He slammed the button down.

A sudden bubbling of the water mid-channel was followed by a loud woosh as the Rockets shot up from their underwater silos. Each Rocket, more than six feet in length, was packed with the explosive equivalent of several Emergency Flares.

All were capable of turning the night skies to brightest day in a pyrotechnic supernova.

And one. Just one, might be lucky enough to connect with the deadly drone and knock it off course. Juan held his breath. 9 of the 10 rockets whizzed safely by the device.

But one hit it. Dead centre.

There was a loud crackling followed by a massive explosion. With the combined C4 explosive and the Rocket, the massive boom from the flying bomb echoed around the harbour valley like Krakatoa erupting. The drone and its explosive package were blown into a thousand pieces that fell like fizzing molten rain into the water below.

The Cultural Attaché, cowering behind the podium, was shaken but unharmed. Everyone on the platform was safe. Juan breathed a sigh of relief and slumped forward on top of the consul desk.

The people on the hillsides clapped and cheered loudly. They'd never seen such good Underwater Fireworks.

In the cold night water Frank did his best to locate Irina. The last thing he could remember was colliding with her and both of them going over the side. A loud explosion somewhere. Then coming-to in the water, trying to stay afloat and get his breath. Irina nowhere to be seen.

He called and called but heard no reply. Taking huge gulps of air, he dived down under the water and searched around. But it was too dark to see very much.

Trying to swim with his hands still tied didn't make it any easier, and after several dives he was exhausted. He stopped and began treading water, trying to catch his breath and get his thoughts together.

The boat was gone. Goran had legged it as soon as the bomb went off. Perhaps Irina had made it back to the craft?

Or maybe she had swum to the shore. It was hard to know. But there was no sign of her here.

He decided to head for the shore himself, before risking passing out again.

His hands still bound, he turned onto his back and began kicking slowly. The stars above twinkled. Rockets flew up and burst in crescendos of light and sound in the clear cobalt night sky. A song began in his head '*Starlight, star bright. First star I see tonight*'.

It was almost sublime, and a sudden calmness came over him. Until he thought again about the drone bomb. Had the device done its deadly deed?

He stopped and looked towards the VIP's platform. It was a good quarter of a mile away, but it was still there. It still looked intact. And in the lights of its lamps he could just make out people moving about. Perhaps the bomb had failed to find its target.

But there had been that huge explosion! He looked again at the podium to make sure his eyes weren't deceiving him. No, still there and looking intact. Then the scene started to fade, like a watercolour painting washing away in the rain, as he drifted into unconsciousness once more.

As he blacked out, he was dimly aware of the sound of a motorboat approaching. Someone was shouting something. His name? He summoned all his strength and held his bound hands aloft. He tried to reply but nothing more than a croak would come out of his mouth. The scene went dark.

He felt himself slipping below the waves.

'NO WAY TO SAY GOODBYE'

It was dark underwater. Then suddenly there was a bright
light shining from above. He saw Irina swimming toward
him, passed the curtains of hanging seaweed and dancing
Medusas. She was a mermaid with a tail. Of course! He
should have known.

No wait, here was another. It was Marisol. She swam up
and joined Irina. Now came a third mermaid. It was Linda,
his late wife. They drew near and were reaching out to him,
smiling and beckoning him to come with them.

He felt a wave of joy and love sweeping over him. The rope
that had bound his wrists was now magically gone. He was
happy to go with them.

He was about to take their hands when, suddenly above
them the light got even brighter. As it did, the Mermaids,
waved, turned and swam away like frightened fish.

One stopped, and looked back. It was Marisol. She was
saying something but he could not quite make it out. Then

he felt himself being drawn up quickly towards the bright light and the words became clear.

'Atención Doctor Tomaso. Lo necesitan en cirugía. Atención Doctor Tomaso.'

He awoke in bed. He opened his eyes and blinked at the brightness of the hospital room. His throat was dry and he needed water. He let out a groan as he tried to move and felt a sharp pain in the back of his skull.

Juan was stood over by the door talking quietly to a nurse. They both turned on hearing him.

'Ah, you have rejoined us in the land of the living.'

Juan came over to the bedside and helped him to sit up. He filled a cup with water from the pitcher on the bedside cabinet and held it for Frank to drink.

He drank greedily. He was parched and there was a revolting taste of blood and stale vomit in his mouth.

He put a hand to his head and felt the bandage wrapped around it. The memories of the night before began to trickle back into his brain. Then the questions came flooding out.

The bomb? Everyone safe? What happened?

Juan told him all was fine. Everyone was safe and he went through the events in order. How he had spotted the drone at the last minute. How he had activated the Underwater Fireworks Rockets and, luckily taken out the device. How the police patrol boat had found Frank unconscious in the water and pulled him to safety. Then a waiting ambulance brought him here to the hospital.

'Don't worry. No permanent damage. Doc says you've got a skull like granite.' Juan looked at the Ward Sister for agreement. She was not given to bedside humour and simply said 'The doctor will need to check you out again, but you should be okay to return home in the morning.'

It was a lot to take in. He still had so many questions. But there was one above all others that he had to know. He was almost scared to ask it. He looked at Juan and whispered 'Irina?'

Juan shook his head slowly 'We picked up the boat and her accomplice, Goran. He didn't get very far. Ran his Yacht into some rocks before he even got out of the channel. Not much of a sailor I think.'

Frank laughed and nodded, then wished he had kept his head still. Juan gave him a sympathetic smile and then continued. 'He told us everything. Not at first of course, but when we told him we would have to hand him over to the Serbian police for interrogation unless he co-operated, he sang like a canary.'

'He told us all about Irina. Said it was all her idea. Her plot to kill the Serbian Attaché. The Fiesta Killer with the red cap. The bomb. Everything.'

He knitted his brow and shook his head. 'We searched the water. Both banks of the Harbour also. No sign of her. No body. Yet. But at daybreak we will have police divers searching. We've got roadblocks out and we'll check every passenger travelling by sea and air. Don't worry, we will find her my friend.'

Somehow Frank doubted it, but simply nodded, wincing, in agreement. He felt bad that part of him didn't want her to get caught. However, he was glad that she had failed in her assassination attempt, and that maybe she was alive somewhere.

He hoisted himself up on his elbows and sat back against the large pillow. He put his hand on Juan's arm and said. 'Well done my friend. You are the hero of the hour.'

Juan shrugged and shook his head. 'No. I was lucky to be in the right place at the right time. It was you who are the hero, Señor Frank. You risked your life to stop that atrocity. It was your excellent detective work that alerted us to the continuing threat of the Fiesta Killer. I shall be making that clear in my report.'

Frank tried to protest, but all that came out was a muffled groan when he shook his head.

The Ward Sister came over and said firmly. 'I think Mr Harmer needs to rest now. Inspector.'

Juan squeezed Frank's shoulder as he went to leave. 'Of course. Get some rest. I must get back to the office and tell my boss the good news. Maybe the successful outcome of this case will be enough to get me out of that blasted basement!'

Frank tried to laugh but he was now feeling exhausted. Perhaps a little nap was in order. He closed his eyes and swiftly sailed into dream world.

The nurse dimmed the lights and quietly closed the door as they left.

Late the following morning the taxi dropped him at the end of the short road that led past Marisol's and to his house. Despite a few reservations and some stern advice about taking it easy, the doctor had given him the all-clear to return home.

He could have come via the ambulance that was available, but did not want to draw attention from his neighbours. They would be talking about it for weeks.

They probably would anyway when they read about the explosive events of the previous night in the papers, especially if his name was mentioned.

Of course, the head bandage was a bit of a giveaway. The fishing hat he had borrowed from a doctor did not cover it very well.

Strange! The shutters of Marisol's lounge window were open. That was not the way she had left them. He knew as he had been feeding her fish and watering her plants while she was away.

The gate was also ajar. That could have been the pool cleaner or postman of course. But still. He pushed it all the way open with his cane and walked slowly up the path to the front door, peering through the lounge window as he did so, trying to see between the slats of the Venetian blinds.

Was that movement in there? Yes. There was someone there! Someone in Marisol's house.

Marisol? He hoped that it was. He wanted to see her and was in no condition to tackle a burglar.

Shaking a little. Not so much from his weakened state but from anticipation. He rang the doorbell. But to cover all the bases, just in case there *was* a burglar he had his walking stick raised at the ready.

After a brief pause and some muffled voices inside, the door was opened. And there was Marisol. Several emotions seemed to flash across her face at once when she saw him, but laughter got the better of her. He looked such a sight!

Standing there, cane raised, head bandaged, unshaven, wearing an ill-fitting blue tracksuit that he had borrowed from an orderly (his own clothes being the victim of the seawater, blood and vomit) and all topped off with a fishing hat adorned with lures and hooks, she could not help but laugh out loud.

He realised how he must have looked and said, 'Don't ask. It's a long story.'

She was laughing and crying as she hugged him.

Despite his sore head, all he wanted to do was hold her as tight as he could and never let her go. He looked into her eyes. No words were needed. They could have embraced like that forever, but a cough from someone else in the hallway, brought them back to reality.

He looked up and saw a woman standing there who bore a close resemblance to Marisol but was much younger and, by the looks of it, very pregnant.

Marisol spoke first 'Ah. Yes.' She turned and made the introductions.

'Frank, I would like you to meet my daughter. Maria. She is coming to live with me here in Menorca.'

Frank couldn't believe his ears. He smiled at the young woman and said 'Hi Maria. Good to meet you.'

Just to be sure had heard it right he asked 'So you are back for good?'

She kissed him on the cheek and taking him by the hand into the house said 'Yes. I am back for good.'

Later that evening Marisol prepared one of her special meals for them all. She was an excellent cook as Frank had already discovered. Afterwards, they sat around the kitchen table sipping wine and chatting. Frank told her the story of the exciting events that had transpired in her absence.

He glossed over one or two details concerning his 'friendship' with Irina.

She told him some of what had transpired in Madrid and mentioned that her daughter had agreed to come and stay with her for a while in Menorca. She did not go into more detail beyond that, and Frank considered it her private family business so did not press her further on the subject.

A little while later Maria expressed a desire to experience a Menorcan Fiesta. She had heard so much about them from Marisol, who had promised to take her to one.

Marisol added that the Cala'n Porter Fiesta, the last of the season, was coming up soon and she could take her to that. She asked Frank if he would like to accompany them.

He was strangely quiet for a while. She asked 'You *do* like Fiestas, don't you?'

A thousand possible answers ran through Frank's mind from the whimsical to the downright sarcastic. But then he looked at her face. Her honest and lovely face.

All he said was 'It will be my pleasure.'